McGlue

Cover image and design by Kathryn Fabrizio
Book design by Rebecca Wolff

Published in the United States by Fence Books
Science Library, 320 University at Albany
1400 Washington Avenue, Albany, NY 12222

www.fenceportal.org

Fence Books are printed in Canada by The Prolific Group and
distributed by Small Press Distribution and Consortium Book Sales
and Distribution.

Library of Congress Cataloguing in Publication Data
Moshfegh, Ottessa [1981- ]
McGlue/Ottessa Moshfegh

Library of Congress Control Number: 2014945617

ISBN 13: 978-1-934200-85-8

First Edition
10 9 8 7 6 5 4 3 2

Fence Books are published in partnership with the University at
Albany and the New York State Writers Institute, and with invaluable
support from the New York State Council on the Arts and the
National Endowment for the Arts.

# McGlue
## Ottessa Moshfegh

The Fence Modern Prize in Prose
Selected by Rivka Galchen

FENCE
BOOKS

"The young men were born
with knives in their brain."

RALPH WALDO EMERSON
*Life and Letters in New England*
(1867)

## Zanzibar

I wake up.

My shirtfront is stiff and bibbed brown. I take it to be dried blood and I'm a dead man. The ocean air persuades me to doubt, to reel my head in double, triple takes towards my feet. My feet are on the ground. It may be that I fell face first in mud. Anyway, I'm still too drunk to care.

"McGlue!"

A wrathful voice calls out from the direction of sunshine, ship sails hoisting, squeaks of wood and knots, tight. I feel my belly buckle. My head. Just last spring I cracked it jumping from a train of cars—this I remember. I get back down on my knees.

Again, "McGlue!"

This McGlue. It sounds familiar.

A hand grips my shirt and pokes at my back, steers me to the plank and I get on, walking somehow. The ship is leaving. I puke and hold on to the side of the stern and belch bile for a bit watching the water rush past, until land is out of sight. It's peaceful for a small while after. Then something inside me feels like dying. I turn my head and cough. Two teeth skip from my mouth and scatter across the deck like dice.

Eventually I am put to bed down under. I fish around my pockets for a bottle and find one.

"McGlue," says the cabin boy, the sissy, "hand that shit over here."

I swig it back. Some spills down my neck and wets my soiled collar. I let the empty bottle fall to the floor.

"You're bleeding," says the fag.

"So I am," I say, pulling my hand away from my throat. It's dark, rummy blood, I taste it. Must be mine, I think. I think of what use it may have if I get thirsty later. Fag looks worried. I don't mind that he unbuttons my shirt, don't even beat his hands away as he steers my neck one way, then the other. Too tired. Inspection time. He says he finds no holes in me to speak of. "Ah ha," I tell him. Fag's face has a weird sneer, and he looks a little scared and hovers there over me, red hair tucked carefully into a wool cap, a dot of sweat sitting in the trivet of his upper lip just below his little nose. He looks me in the eye, I'd say, with some fear.

"No touch," I say, ruffling the blanket back up. It's a grey-and-red striped blanket that smells of lambs' milk. I hold it over my face while Fag goes about. It's good here under the blanket. My breath shows in the dark. So dark I could almost sleep.

My mind travels the cold hills of Peru where I got lost one night. A fat woman fed me milk from her tit and I rode a shaggy dog back down along a river to the coast. Johnson was there with the captain, waiting. That was trouble. Hit warm with the rum now I close my eyes.

"What have you done?" says the captain next time I open them. The blanket is stripped away like a whip. Saunders removes my shoes. I hear the boat creak. Someone walks down the hall ringing a bell for supper. The captain stands there by the cot. "We want to hear you say it," says the captain. I feel sick and tired. I fall asleep again.

✧

They are moving mouths. Saunders and the fag stand by the door. Fag holds a bottle, Saunders dangles keys.

"Gimme." My voice breaks. I can breathe, hear. He passes the bottle over.

"You killed Johnson," says Saunders.

I get a good half the bottle down and steady my neck, fold my shoulders back. I feel my jaw let go, look down, remembering blood. My shirt is gone.

"Where's my shirt."

"Did you really do it?" says the fag. "Officer Pratt says he saw you. Drunk at the pub in Stone Town. Then run away to the dock just before they found him in the alley."

"Trash, it's cold. All possessed till takers of this anti-fogmatico, thank you, faggot," I say. Drink.

"They found him stabbed in the heart dead, man," says Saunders, gripping the keys, eyebrows smarting.

"Who has a brick in a hat, Saunders? Quit it, now. It's keeping me all-overish. Is there food?" The fag takes the empty bottle from where I lay it on the blanket. I feel like dreaming. "Where's your freckles, Puck? Let's trade places."

They aren't talking to me anymore.

"Food, man. Shit." I'm completely awake now. In one glance I take in the room: placards, grey-painted wood walls, wire hooks, some hung-up duck and Guernsey frocks, a grey, shield-shaped mirror. Sunlight hazes in, block-style, speckled with white dust. The shadows of men on deck pass along the walls through the small rectangular windows up high above my cot. An empty cot on either side of me. A whine and creak of ship and ocean. I yearn for ale and a song. This is home—me down in the heart of the drifting vessel, wanting, going somewhere.

Saunders and Fag pass words and go out and I hear Saunders lock the door and I protest with, "Come back and smile, Saunders. Give me the goods, what's up?" and nothing happens.

It's not the first time I've been in the hole on this trip. Will be made to work the pump well each morning and darn sails like an old maid once I'm well again. I think of my mother as I imagine her always at the loom through the nailed-down windows of the mill, me a wee tip-toed kid, fingers hoisting my eyes barely above the horizon of the window ledge, watching my stoop-backed, prim, high-nosed mom at work, and watching her again that night at the table in our little house, calling me and brother "good boys," pushing crumbs, counting coins and coughing, my sisters in bed already, my mother's pale, tuckered out hair splayed across her back. All the stars outside just sitting there. The cold rinse of Salem night after running hot all day. I'd throw a rock at a window if I could, if I had one. Did Saunders say Johnson was in unkeeps? I'll get up and see about it.

I get up. My head thwarts around and I see nothing, then I see stars. Saunders called Johnson dead, I think. I greet the cot again, blind. Saunders will come back with Johnson and have a laugh. Until then I'll ride my cogitations out through the stabbing pains in my skull, the licking waves. Most likely I'll doze then wake up to bread and butter and hot beans and whiskey and it'll be night and we'll be halfway to China and they'll say "Hit the well, McGlue," like after my last bout. I try to remember the port of call I got this wet in.

Zanzibar.

Think of someplace you'd like to go.

I can see again. I take my lids between my fingers and hold them open, take a colt-step towards the mirror. A bit closer and I stumble. A rope is tied around my ankle and bound to the bedpost.

I call out, and my voice makes me ill to hear it. Get back down to the cot, McGlue. Yes, thank you. The stars come out. I look for the moon, but it eludes me. I can't find or measure my way. Drift, drift. If I just close my eyes I'll get there.

I sleep some more.

## Indian Ocean

I wake with fever. I know fever because there's a wet rag folded on my brow. The fag attends me bedside with a book in his lap, one leg swinging from a crabapple–shaped knee. My arms are tied to my thighs, ears shut up, face bandaged around and there's water dripping through the cracks in the deck ceiling and when I breathe I taste a harsh kick of lye and shit. On the dropped-down table slat there's an opened bottle of pickled cabbage and a cake of bread. I look up. The drops of deckwater fall in my eyes and burn. Fag wields a pale wooden tenon in his hand, arm hovering above my head motherly almost.

I open my mouth to curse.

But Fag sticks the tenon lengthwise between my teeth. I rattle around a bit.

"It's what you got, McGlue," Fag says, holding down my neck.

I'm thirsty so I look him in the eye as best I can.

"We can't give you anymore, so don't even ask," is his answer.

He thinks he's got something over me. I let him have it and rattle around some more. With difficulty I use my tongue to taste the roof of my mouth and get salt-air and shit. It's not good. I'd like something sweet about now. There was a little outpost in Borneo that sold wine made out of honey I remember. That was good. The girls there stood around fanning themselves with silver plates, tits and nipples set above tight chainmail vests. Those girls' hips, narrow like young boys', hopped a firm beat between my hands when I willed it, like they were somehow

inside my mind, listening. I sat in the shade and I took them into
the road to dance when it cooled down and I felt like dancing.
Johnson, too. Then "Keep back," he'd said, trotting off, "watch for the
fat one, yell 'pig' if you see him come," pulling one of the girls behind
the jungle curtain back aways and I'd continue to dance and keep my
hands on the girl's hips and when the fat one came I just grabbed
my pistol from my boot and shot it at the stars. The girls loved it,
screaming and running, then laughing and creeping back from
behind the dark palm fronds with their hands over their mouths.
The fat one holding his belly nods to the fresh bottle on the little
stool they use as a table. Forget Johnson, the worried, shameful rat.
I sit and drink and watch the sky. A girl comes and takes my hand
and we dance some more. Johnson shows up again.

"So soon, old man?" I holler, watching him walk back to the
road, his girl slunk back in the dark, chainmail aflash in moonglow.
Always with a girl. He sheds a tear for her, or what he's done, as we
set sail. Always a tear. I laugh. "Why not stay awhile," I used to say,
"build up a nice family, learn the language?" and he'd shove off and
reemerge hours later all cool and fixed, talk to the captain on the
virtues of clippers over cutters and be asking how he'd got in the
racket and so on, starry-eyed. Make me sick. I watch the girls now
in a line waving goodbye from the shore, picture them standing
along the crack in the ceiling of this darkening room, eyes ashimmer
like drops of water, and I rattle on.

Drink, please.

I've been this sick before.

"Shit," I try to say, but the tenon's got my tongue again. I look at Fag. His eyes are on his lap, reading lines.

If Fag won't give me rum then let me suck the brine from that cabbage at the very least, I think. I get myself on my right side, planning something. Fag gets up and digs his elbow in the nook of my waist. I spit the tenon out onto the floor. Blood leaks from my mouth.

"Happy now, fagger?" I slurp. My voice hurts my head. My head, I seem to recall, has a big crack in it.

"Count a blessing, McGlue. Next stop's Mac Harbour, where we ought to just set you right down with the rest of the cons."

"Pleased if you do," I say, and slam my head back against the cot. The effect is good: a sharp taste of blood in the back of my throat and I see black for a while, then white. Sleep again.

## Macquarie Harbour, Tasmania

We're docked and most mates are ashore but blackies locked in the next cabin are snoring. Then I hear one pour something in a cup. I'm awake. I rub my wrists rough up against my hips and get the ropes undone, get up and drag the foot of my cot to the wall and take a breath. I see a canteen on the dropped-down table. So I drag the cot that way and grab it and drink till it's empty. Just water. It glaciers down my tubes the opposite of piss on snow and I double over and curse—my first words in days. The blackies mumble. Then I drag the cot to the wall again and step up on it, look through the high window over the deck. It's blue everywhere. The sky is blue. The clouds are blue. The ocean's blue. The slow zig-zag of a seagull sways in my eyes in such a way they start to water. Am I crying? If this side of the ship was facing land I think I'd puke for wanting. Any other day I'd be purchasing a tin of tobacco, taking some in my gums quick then more in a pipe, squint, drum my chest, yell at Johnson to get on. How many hours till the ship's loaded, I'd find out. We'd take a ride to town, see what they've got to get into here. A country full of murderers and thieves must have good stuff, I'm thinking. Blood wine, I'm thinking. Whiskey made from ladies' fingers. Some kind of strong snuff from bad plants used to treat the blackhearts in lock-up. Roasted meats. Pies filled with sugar plums, rats, brandy. I can bet I know what the mates would be saying. Nasty, wrench-pussied women all about. I am starving.

"Starving!" I yell out to the sea.

They said I've done something wrong? Johnson must be angry and won't come down to make it right. Not yet. And they've just left me down here to starve. Haven't had a drop in days more so. They'll see this inanition and be so damned they'll fall to my feet and pass up hot cross buns slathered in fresh butter and beg I forgive them. All of them: Johnson, Pratt, captain, Saunders, the fagger, the entire world one by one. Like a good priest I'll pat their heads and nod. I'll dunk my skull into a barrel of gin.

I feel happy imagining my hand on Johnson's bowed head, the black, gleaming hair through my fingers. I'd twirl it around like a little girl does braids, pinch his cheeks, let some of my hungryman drool drip down on his face, unhook the frog in my throat, "Johnny," I'll say. "A toast." Two cups of ale up and down our mouths and our seamen's beards are full of foamy slaver. It was like that in Salem, nights we waited to leave port. The red in Johnson's cheeks blooms like flowers every time he swallows, then fades again while he talks. His hair, black and slick as hot tar, never flails or wanders from where it lies, no matter what the wind or rain. "Pretty," they say. He called me "Soaplocker" for how I wore my hair when we first met: so long in front I'd wrap it around my ears and it'd hold. He says he took me for a kid like fifteen the night he found me and thought himself a real hero.

I have to laugh. The first time I saw Johnson I thought he was one of those asshole Charlies you hear engage with kids out in the woods for a few cents a suck or whatnot. I know these types well.

"You think," he'd said, "that rum will keep you from freezing the night?"

I had my hat over my face, bottle between my knees, slowly melting my ass into a seat of snow propped up dead-tired against a tree. Johnson sat on a horse.

"Get going," I said. A Charlie or not, I didn't care. I'd made it a few days into a jag by that night, somewhere between New Haven and Orange. I was never going home again. I could see the ice-paved beach through the moonlit trees. I had another whole, full bottle—a double pint— in my coat pocket, and some money left. I was good. That was my thinking.

But Johnson wouldn't leave. His horse reared up and he pulled and steered her back, both his breath and horse snort steaming out like ghostly spirits leaving their bodies, like some child's scary poem. I tried to laugh but my face had frozen. I remember that.

"You'll die out here," said Johnson. "Let me take you into town."

"Go fuck," I told him. He acted like he didn't hear and steered the horse around some more.

"Puck, you say?" he said. I took a drink. "A boy's read Shakespeare comes to spend the night on ice. Aw…" He slapped his horse's rump. "Get on that, Nicky Bottom."

He acted like a fag but didn't look like one. A joke, I thought. Making fun of me, what I'd expect him to be. He leaned down and put his hand in my face for me to take hold of. He asked where I came from, and when I'd said, "Salem," he laughed.

"I was born there," he said, pulling me up.

I'd been hammered down bad before and by this time—I was twenty-two, twenty-three—I knew that I was doomed. I'd accustomed myself to that most of all. For some reason, though, I went along: I got up on the horse and grabbed the saddle strap where I could and we rode. It must have been just as cold on that horse as it was sitting back there in the snow. But he could be right, Johnson. He may have saved my life.

We headed south and rode all through the night as I recall. Johnson said around Stratford I leaned my head up on his shoulder and snored. I woke up, must have been days later, in Mamaroneck in the afternoon, head on a clean white tablecloth, smelling fish fry.

Johnson stood by the stove with his back to me and his arm around a girl. The girl brought a plate to the table. There was a brown fried fish. "Nick here won't eat that, sister," he said. "Give him potatoes. I think that's all he can stomach for now, that right?"

I nodded.

Johnson came and sat and ate the fish with a silver fork, one hand in his lap.

"McGlue," I told him.

He gave me his hand again.

Fag unlocks the door hours later. It's turned grey, early evening. He's wearing a funny green sweater. He leaves a crate of oranges on the dropped-down, then comes and stands over me. I fold my hands.

"Captain says to give you food. There's some oranges. I'll send you down a plate later. And I guess some ale. But captain said no more rum. You've got a big hole in your head, McGlue."

I touch the crack with my finger. My ears ring. I wake up more, it's like a bright, sunny day and nowhere to go. All the more rum I'll need, I think.

"You need to go, you go here," he says, going back out to the hall and carrying in a big tin bucket. He sets it carefully by the bed.

"Many thanks, faggot," I say. "Throw me an orange."

He selects one and tosses it softly into my open palms. Nice little fag, I think. Good boy, I'm thinking, watching him leave and lock the door. I pierce the dimpled orange peel with my thickened, yellow thumbnail. The perfume rouses the hairs in my nose, making my eyes water. I sniff deep. My head fills with the sour spray, scratching an itch deep in my brain. It's good. I take a bite, peel and all. It's not good. This is me now: puking fruit into a bucket already half full of blackie piss and shit.

I lay back down and close my eyes. Soon there will be hot food. The thought makes my stomach turn. A mug of cold ale more like it. I'll sleep till then, think of Shanghai. The so-often swept and scoured plaza. The great clock. The perfect skin of the girl. No variation. You could paint her in three colors: yellow, black and red.

Fag wakes me in the dark with a cold plate of hash and digs a fork into my fist. "No ale," he says. "Captain's orders." Still just remembering my name, what man I am, I sit up in my cot and eat as best I can.

*South Pacific, a month later*

I've been studying a Walch's Tasmanian almanac, memorizing pages, not to let my mind-muscle go to flub like my arms and legs have after almost a month, I guess, of lying down here, imprisoned. Sometimes when I look down, a less-thinking part of me looks up at the shapes and curves of my flesh and bone which have taken on a kind of pale and pretty shiftiness, like a young country girl in winter. I lift the sheets and stare and stare. Well, it's a good game to play when I'm too bored to think. My mind wanders watching it rise and tarry. If they give me food in the morning and it's not too cold, I tend to pass the time aloud, sing the songs I learned in school, talk to an invisible Johnson, have a laugh or two, get some soul out. I've asked Saunders and Fag to provide me with some diversions. "Let me walk around the ship. You think I'll swim away?" I say. They tell me I should be happy with what I've got to read —three letters raised on the blue glass bottle of O-I-L. They don't know about the almanac. They keep saying I've killed Johnson.

Without Johnson around to have look-aftering, and all these mates down on me as a killer, I miss the rum. I am beginning to hear what they say I've done. Fag says I should lay here quietly and pray. I tell him I'm thirsty. I flip the blanket down and lift my johns.

"Fagger," I say. "If I was thirsty, would you afford this?"

I see his eyes twitch, the fag.

"You smell like a dead horse's ass, McGlue." His scoff is so huffy, I laugh.

I look down at the lovely alabaster ridged cliffs and valleys of my body, scribbled with little light brown curls down into a shag of darkened, wet and heady hell. A tall mug of port would be good. I'd kiss you, I think. It makes itself known, unshies itself from the dark down there.

"Hello," I say to it. It rises.

Fagger's watching.

"The fag'll have none of you then," I say, and lick my hand.

"Fag," I say, reaching down to it, "stay with me."

He sees well the game I'm playing. He stays.

That evening he brings me a hogshead of ale.

The next morning, a bottle of the good stuff.

I'm good again. I don't read the almanac as much. Hell hides in the ditch and my eyes are dry.

*South Pacific*


Captain comes in. He's got on a new jet black felt hat.

"What's worse, McGlue? You want to confess today?"

"I didn't do it," I say.

"And you don't recall."

"No recollection."

"Show me your hands," he says, and I stretch them out towards him best I can. They warble and drift from side to side. He steadies one between his two warm palms. Then he slaps it, hard. A naughty child. I don't laugh.

"Word's been sent to your mother, McGlue. You'll be tried in Salem, most likely in the first degree. Or even second degree. The greatest degree if you want to know what I think you're due." That idiot. He wrenches his face and looks away and sways back on his heels and tries again to look me in the face but can't and wrenches his face again. He resembles a drowned man: doughy-faced, unbearded, eyes bulging and colorless, veins showing clearly at his throat. "You think it's one big gag, don't you. Lie down here all day, do no work, think you've got the world in a book. Drunken trash," he calls me. "I never saw what Johnson said you'd be any good for, and I was right. Don't want to think what his family would have to say to you. Why would anyone? People are gonna want to know why you did it, McGlue. Better start thinking real hard. What have you been thinking all this time?"

I fold my hands and sit up a little in the cot. I just look at him like, *What*?

"We'll be home in a month," he says. He comes a bit closer and looks down at my head from above, I guess at the crack. Inspection time. On his way out he catches scent of the piss and shit bucket, and looks at the fag and cocks his chin at it, and goes out with his head down. His chin is gutty and flubbed like a fish that way. I wonder who would ever want to fuck such a man.

Things get slow down here.

There was a little Hindu man sitting cross-legged in the market in Calcutta waving a sword around his head. Johnson elbowed me at the sight of him, so we stopped and watched him put the blade down his throat, all the way till the handle was just sitting on his teeth. Some men came and the little man ran off, his head still thrown back, moving nimbly like a little lizard.

I asked Johnson how he could've survived such impalement.

"It's all empty in there, Nicky," he told me, drumming his chest. "Like a tunnel." Then he knocked on my head. "You may be just clear of junk up here instead," he said.

What I have been thinking, captain, is what is exempt from import tax in one country is what I'd like to stick through the crack in my skull to start to fill it: hay, oranges, lemons, pineapples, cocoa nuts, grapes, green fruit, and vegetables of every variety, and linseed oil cake. Horses, pigs, poultry, dogs, and living animals of every description, except cattle and sheep. Corks, bark, firewood, logwood, and dyewoods. Copper or yellow metal, rod bolts or sheathing, and copper and yellow metal nails. Felt for sheathing, oakum and junk, pitch, tar, and resin. Sail canvas, boats, and boat oars.

I fill my head with ships' blocks, binnacle lamps, signal lamps, compasses, shackles, sheaves, deadeyes, rings and thimbles, dead lights, anchors, and chain cables of every description, and galvanized iron wire rope. Lime juice and ice. Printed books, music, and newspapers, maps, charts, globes, and uncut cardboard, millboard, and pasteboard. Ink, printing presses, printing type, and other printing materials. Passengers' baggage or cabin furniture arriving in the colony at any time within three months before or after the owner thereof. Tablets, memorial windows, harmoniums, organs, bells, and clocks specially imported for churches or chapels. Hides and skins of every description, raw and unmanufactured. Veneers of all sorts. Rattans, split or unsplit.

Carriage shafts, spokes, naves, and felloes. School slates and slate pencils, slates for roofing, and slates and stone for flagging. Marble, granite, slate, or stone in rough block.

Soda ash, caustic soda, and silicate of soda. Cotton waste, woollen waste, candle cotton, wool, flax, hemp, tow, and jute, unmanufactured. Specimens of natural history, mineralogy, or botany. Gold dust, gold bars, bullion, and coin. Coir bristles and hair unmanufactured. Broom heads and stocks, partly manufactured for brushmaking purposes. Jars of glass or of earthenware, specially imported for jam. Rod bar hoop sheet plate and pig iron and piglead share moulds and mould boards. Epsom salts, citric acid, sulphuric acid, muriatic acid, carbolic acid. Hair cloth for hopkilns. Wines and spirits.

Captain.

What's true?

We stayed a night in Mamaroneck, and though I'd have liked to get out and have a run at a grog shop, Johnson said we had to get up early to ride into the city, and laid out for me a set of his old clothes across the back of a chair: heavy brown trousers, a clean shirt, vest and woolen frock coat.

"New Haven is good for two things," said Johnson, undressing for bed. "Sam Colts and cotton gin." I watched him from where I stood, warming myself by the fire. His arms were thin and finely wrought. Hands red and afog in what I could only think what must be beauty. "I'm done," he said, getting into bed. "New York is full of rich people, money, and wine. You just have to learn how to not take too much or you'll get shut down."

I stood there with my hands in my pockets. I was thinking he was a ride somewhere and another few meals until I got there.

"Who's the girl?" I asked him.

"An old maid," was his answer.

I stood there some more and watched him rub his eyes in a cracked mirror on the bedside table. "What you want me here for?"

"You got a gun?" he asked.

"Yeah."

"And you haven't shot me yet," he said.

"No."

He threw a blanket at the rug by the fire and rolled over.

In the morning we found that Johnson's trousers were too long on me and he had the girl hem them while I sat in my long johns by the fire and he got the horse ready.

## North Sea, south of Long Fourties

There is a storm in the night and the boat rocks. Mates clamber up and down the hall and across the deck, hollering over the wind and rain. Raise the sails, furl the sails, repair the rigging, I remember all that. I stand on the cot to look out the window, wipe my face, watch the lightning flash through the white tower of flags, whipping crazy, the bow flying high, chair scraping along the floor behind me, the black seas all around. The ship tilts and rain spills in through the window onto the cot. I get up and drag the cot up against the door. This kind of dizzy makes sense when I walk. The piss and shit bucket I wedge in the corner. I'd like a smoke. I tip the cot to get the water off and lay back down. This is like high seas. The best part. I close my eyes, let the room spin.

"If you can't sleep, think of things you like to eat, things you see walking down a road, girls' names. Say them in your head, again and again, until you're done."

"I'm never done, Johnson," I tell him. "It's what I always need, one more."

"Johnson, Johnson, Johnson, Johnson..."

## Bay of Biscay

This is me: elbows point out the sides, fists in pits, wide step with leg
outstretched and knee high and foot flexed out, back arching. Then
knee bent and foot coming down just barely an inch in front of the
other, back caving in, elbows straightening, arms hang down, fingers
splay and shake towards the floor, ass stretched back, head up, I close
my eyes. This is how I walk. This is how I'll walk from now on.

I sit on the chair.

It's so boring.

I yell "Fag" real loud. I'll ask him to send me in some blackies
to play with. They're the most fun anyhow. But Fag doesn't come. I
get up again. Take a drink from the canteen. It's weak whiskey. Not
enough. I whistle. I think I'd like to be a conjurer. I shut my eyes.

"Like we saw in Istanbul, with the smoke, and the curtain?"

"That fat Russian girl?"

"Yeah. She was pretty."

"No," I spit. "A real conjurer, Johnson. Make something show
up, just like that." I snap my fingers. "No smoke."

He strikes a match on the underside of the dropped-down
and throws me a bottle, lights his pipe. He looks worried about
something. I watch his eyes.

"What is it?" I ask.

"It's so quiet down here," he says, testing the cot with his knee.
"Wouldn't you prefer a mate to board with?" His one eye's squinched
from the smoke. He sits.

"Who's gonna board with me? They all think I'm a killer."

"Well, who'd you want to board with?"

"The wizard they crushed with rocks in Salem Prison way back."

"How'd they crush him?"

"They piled rocks on him. Boulders. Till his tongue and eyeballs squirted out his head."

"Was he a real wizard?"

"If he wasn't, he died an idiot."

"And you, McGlue?"

"No, I'm not an idiot, thanks."

"Well, come on, let's do something."

"There's nothing to do, Johnny."

Johnson puffs his pipe, leans back cross-legged on the cot, doesn't move his head.

"Keep it still," he says, and works his mouth around like a horse and turns a bit pale it seems from not breathing and he shuts his eyes, like dead play. I just stand there with my hands on the back of the chair and wait for him to laugh. We used to do this: drunk at the bottom of the stairs or fell from a tree, punched hard in a brawl, hurled from a horse, he or I'd just lie there unmoving long enough to make the other one shake us. Then we'd laugh. "What, you thought I was dead? Idiot." So I stand and wait for Johnson. But instead of a laugh what comes out of his mouth when it opens is a pillar of smoke the size of a full-grown man, and the smokeman's got a little smokedog on a rope, and they hover there, like they're waiting to cross a road. Johnson takes a deep breath and steadies himself, pinching his eyes shut hard, then opening them and shaking his face out. We watch the smoke. The man's got on a kind of loose brown woven cloak and a burndled, ugly hat, long hair. The dog looks not so old.

"You McGlue?" the man looks at Johnson. His voice scrapes lightly, sourcelessly through the cold, thick ocean air. Johnson shakes his head.

"I've got your dog," says the man. And sticks out his fist with the rope, the end looped. "He's yourn yet," he says. I take hold of the rope. The dog jumps up and scrambles its paws at my knees. I feel nothing.

"Thank the man," says Johnson.

"Thank you," I say.

Johnson laughs. The dog's pissing on my foot. Johnson's laugh is mean and sounds made-up.

These dreams make my heart hurt.


When I was a boy—six, seven, eight—I had a little dog.

"You think it's gonna live forever?" somebody asked me.

I'm quiet.

I went for a walk to the store on Buff to see if he'd sell me a drink.

"Mom gave me this to buy a dram of rye." I set the coin on the counter.

"A dram?" His moustache had bits of brown bread in it. There was glass in the bottom of the counter where I could see my legs reflected. Behind my legs there were pipes lined up in a row. Some of the pipes were made of bones. There were red candies on a sheet of paper. Each one had a daub of red painty stuff on the paper beneath it. Also taffy. My little dog licked my shoe.

"You like sweets?"

I shook my head and took the bottle.

I can remember this, and I pass the schoolyard with doggy. Teacher's black bonnet like a big black bug. It's windy there. She waves and pulls a strand of hair from her mouth, keeps walking. I trade the rope from one hand to the other, feel the little bottle in my pocket. The windy warm autumn air feels nice. Doggy barks at the dust a small horse kicks up on Howard Street, and I don't like it on Howard Street anyhow. Good boy. Howard Street is where they bury dead men. And there's the jail, red brick and lots of pokey chimneys sticking into the clean blue sky above it. Maybe I'll go up Howard Street and just see. I think this is where they bury just old men. Not young boys. I won't go out that way. Nobody I know is buried here. I try to see through the windows of the jail but they are crisscrossed, and dark. Doggy fumbles on the rope and squeals. I don't like it. I turn the other way towards the commons and try a happy song in my head.

I feel the little bottle in my pocket and whistle once I reach the grass.

There's Dwelly throwing a ball. There's Rich.

"That your dog, McGlue?"

"Ya, it's mine."

"Can it do tricks?"

"Sit," I say. "Sit down."

My little dog's tail twitches fast and it pees and its ears flop and it shudders back and looks scared and I bend down to pet it.

"Dog's a bitch, Mick," says Rich.

"Ya," says Dwelly.

Dwelly throws the ball in the air. It's getting almost dark.

I pull the bottle out and show them.

We walk down to Derby Street, past all the big fancy houses, the fire in the glass lanterns on every corner, and pass the little bottle back and forth. It's gone too soon. Rich has got to go. I go home with Dwelly to play more. He lives just down the road from me. I tie the dog to a post out front. It cries and I don't care.

The boat's been steady. Fag comes and goes without saying much. A
blackie comes now and again to empty the piss and shit pot. I try to rile
him up to make a joke or two, but he won't have it. He holds his palms
up around his face and sticks his tongue out. It's meant to scare me
and it does. I'll just wait until I get back home to think ahead. For now,
there's much to remember.

Like New York.

There was a cold mist across the lawn and fat sheep along a little
hill and a few men on horses and a big sprawl of land one way and
another way and the grass and trees rubbed out for roads and little
houses, and rivers on either side which I could see in spots where the
mist cleared and if I squinted. There were pigs sleeping in a little gutter
by the edge of the park. A sign on a post said PARADE.

We'd got to Manhattan Island early in the morning and right
away Johnson found a man to buy his horse. I pawed up the hill and sat
with my back against the tree. There was no snow there but the ground
was frozen. I watched Johnson sell his horse. He didn't pat her on the
neck or anything to say goodbye. Just put the money in his pocket and
walked up the hill.

"Down there is where the boats and folk live," Johnson pointed.
"Let's go find my cousin." We set off down the hill and towards the
southern end of the island, Johnson with his head bowed and hat tall
and coat flared, hands in pockets and cheeks aglow with pink, and then

trotting down a wide lane with few people on the streets so early, turning his head just barely to take in the place as though he already knew where he was and where he was going, and he hurried on and on, me trundling behind, vision spotted white from sunshine, legs like deadwood at first from the long day and night's ride then numb with cold and huffing smoky air and no hat and I said, "Johnson," but I didn't stop because he walked too fast, but I was cold and thirsty so I ran up next to him and said, "I need a drop quick if we're to keep like this all day," and he stopped and nodded, which I didn't expect. I expected him to shove me off, but he stopped and nodded and looked up and took me by the collar and ruffled it up around my neck. A sign said BURNT MILL POINT. How I remember this, God knows. I looked in Johnson's eyes. He stood there facing me a few breaths. Nothing came out of his eyes like I was used to seeing in any man. I felt some fear.

"We have to get that mustache off you," Johnson said.

We were out by the docks by now and it was so cold and windy we took a corner inward and down an avenue marked D where the streets were filled with people and carriages and children. We went along and I took a look at the faces: some greased up and pale-eyed and worn and young and others pulled tight and dry and rubbed red with wind and some with scarves on and some with blankets over their shoulders and some sitting in the doorways and some kids rolling a broken cart with two puppies in it and one yelling, "Down theyah," and a row of young ladies in black-and-green dresses lifting their skirts over muddy puddles across the street, holding books under their arms, small gloved hands, and a big uncoated man pulling a bull, another big man beside him with a full orange beard walking backwards, sploshing through the puddles and upsetting an older, white-haired couple stepping slowly, arm-in-arm up the stones and onto a curb into a little alley. The rows of houses were all lined up and touching one another for the most part, and some houses had just a number painted on the glass and some had signs hanging in the windows advertising dry goods or hardware or tailoring or something. As we passed by one brown wooden door, two girls came out in long grey coats with hoods, one carrying a loaf of bread. They both looked Johnson up and down, then at each other, smiling meanly, it seemed. He tipped his hat and turned. Whores. I looked through the window and into the little store: brightly colored tins and jars of jams, big and small breads heaped on high shelves and a lamp burning. An old man leaning against a high counter, turning the pages of a newspaper. A little boy with his back facing, dancing in the blackies' way. I heard his feet clack the floorboards, then Johnson said, "Up there," and we went up the road and turned a few corners onto a street called Clinton.

In the front room of a house a man was selling liquors. We went in and it was suddenly quiet—the noise of the streets and people and horses and bells hushed behind the closed door and the closeness of the booze. The booze, most of all, just sitting there, made it quiet.

"What sort is this?" Johnson asked him.

There were bottles on the shelf. The man had a heavy jowl and buggish, slow-moving eyes.

"Grog shop sells grog," he said. "Dis a friend of yours?" The man was sticking a thumb at me. Johnson gave him the money and made a funny face to make me smile.

"Are you a friend, Nick," he said.

The stuff was sweet like brandy but did a foul, sour number on my tongue. I drank a bottle down and had Johnson pay for a few more and I opened the next one and passed it to Johnson and he took a swig and winced and laughed and passed it back to me, and that was it.

We kept walking. It had warmed a bit. I paid less mind to the people. The street was called Rivington. Johnson slowed. We turned into a small alley and into a barbershop. The place smelled like smoke and laundry soap. A short old man pushed me down into a leather armchair. I took a drink.

A young kid shaved my beard and combed my hair. His fingers were so soft I wondered how he kept from getting cut. I grit my jaw. Johnson sat and spoke with men in rough suits. "We come from up north, on business," I heard him say.

Two men walked in speaking another language. It reminded me of a sad song. The old man in charge bleared loudly, "Git ow!" Then a fat lady came out the back blowing a bugle. The old man scuttled her back away. I smelled cooking cabbage. The two men were gone. The kid slapped my face with a burny salve and pushed me softly up out of the chair. Johnson took a hat off the pole and a bell clanged when we swung through the door. I had a new hat.

In all this I knew I could break off and go wherever I pleased. I had a gun worth a bit and a mind of my own. I didn't break off though. I figured he was paying. I figured, he must be crazy.

We went into a corner store and sat down and Johnson ordered coffee and plates of food and a blackie brought it to us on a tray and Johnson watched me pour what was left of the bottle into the cup after I'd drank all the coffee and then he wiped his mouth and told me why we'd come.

"We're going to go find my cousin," he said. "This is where the people come and this is where the money is and this is where I want to make it because up there there's nothing but old ties, and I'm done with old ties. And you're a good kid, and a drunk, but you just do what I say and you'll make it with me, right?"

"Right," I said, but it didn't feel very right. I didn't want to make it. I wanted to lie down with it and strangle it and kill it and save it and nurse it and kill it again and I wanted to go and forget where I was going and I wanted to change my name and forget my face and I wanted to drink and get my head ruined but I certainly hadn't thought about making it. That wasn't anything I'd ever sought out to do. We walked back out to the docks and to a shipyard where there was much smoke and noise and I stayed back in a tavern with some coins Johnson put in my hand while he went out, he said, to look for his cousin. He came back a few hours later. I was under the table by then, a red-faced short little guy with pig ears by my side asking me what I did for money and me saying, "I sing."

"Have a song," Pig said, coming closer, and Johnson shoved him off and tugged my collar.

"Come," said Johnson. "Can you walk?"

"Piggy back," I said, and circled around. The dark wood planks of floor came up, I tasted sawdust. I slept. That sour brandy taste on my tongue revived me a moment later. I looked up into Johnson's eyes. They sparkled this time. I began to sing a song. And Johnson just sat there with my head in his lap, listening. It wasn't what I'd expected. After one verse I stood up and went with him out the door and toward Clinton where Johnson said there was a boarding house.

"That's where you live now." He pushed me into a bed next to beds full of men and men sitting between the beds playing cards and smoking and passing bottles and sometimes hollering too loud and someone yelping up to tell them to shut it, and the night stilled eventually and I felt Johnson's weight in the bed with me, and it was New York.

In the morning New York was there again, with fog horns and racket from the street and Johnson snoring, and I got up to piss and saw a bottle in an old man's satchel poking out so I nabbed it and drank it and put the empty bottle back and went to find the head.

I feel the boat begin to slow. It must be Lima.

## New York, New York

"Get up," says Johnson.

"How'd you find me here?" He's standing at the foot of my bed, big fancy hat on, the ass. I've never seen him in Five Points before, let alone for the past six weeks.

"I asked where the stinking drunk who sings was sleeping, what do you think?"

"What, are you mayor of Manhattan now?"

"Let's go. This place is full of fleas."

And Johnson's right. This place, Old Brewery sectioned up into little rooms with floors and walls drooping and full of mites and mosquitoes and rats, will make you itch just to look at it. It makes me thirsty. I've been here for some time, wake in the afternoons, taking some money off a fool downstairs in cards, drink, go out, uptown, make a plan, make up my future staring through the wrought-iron gates of Gramercy Park, then forget it, back down to Five Points, hit up Abbott family in the next room for food, bounce a baby on my knee, go down to Little Water oyster saloon, wake up the next day, do it again.

"I read about you in the papers," says Johnson, lacing up my boots.

He hands me a rolled up newspaper. I try to read as I stumble down the stairs.

*We understand a scuffle took place in our streets on Saturday last between an unknown young northerner and Silas B.*

*Woolcutt in which the latter gentleman came out minus one lip. In consequence of this calamity we fear he will not be able to give quite as much lip in our streets hereafter as has been his custom. And although the young man may have acquired a superabundance of lip by the operation, he certainly cannot be justified in adopting this method of shirting an opponent, or abating a misstep, and may possibly find himself minus his liberty of operating beyond the walls of a certain ugly tenement, where something more than lip service will be required of him, should he not tame his ways.*

"You think I care?" I ask.

Johnson's got me out the door already. He pushes me into a buggy. I continue to read.

*A black man was knocked down and robbed night before last in the vicinity of the Five Points.*

"This one wasn't me either," I say.

*Celia Riddle, yellow girl, of Bayard Street was found at the Five Points, drunk and disorderly and wanting to fight. Committed.*

*Hannah Fowle, alias Donnelly of 313 Pearl Street was brought in beastly drunk, and swore it was her husband that was drunk, and not herself. Committed.*

*Bernard Lawless, just from New Orleans, was brought*
*in drunk from the oyster house of a man named Smith for*
*attempting to leave a child there, which he brought with him,*
*and swore that he had never seen before, though it was his child.*
*He was fined $1 which he paid and was discharged.*
*William Shilleto was tried for stealing 7 Britannia*
*spoons and a silk handkerchief of Ramsay Crook, in Beekman*
*Street, which were found in his trunk. Judgment suspended, on*
*condition of going to sea.*

"You idiot," says Johnson. He turns a page and points. The carriage clunks along Second Avenue. I haven't looked at who's reining the horse.

*Nick Bottom of Five Points, believing he was pursued as*
*a stowaway on the White Plains line, having boarded first at*
*Bowery—some say he was fleeing a mad Roach Guard boy owed*
*a gambling debt—jumped near the Harlem River very barely*
*missing the water but suffering a break to his skull which landed*
*him in Demilt Dispensary downtown last Thursday. No charges.*

"I'm taking you home."

I stand to grab the driver's shoulder but Johnson pulls me back down by the seat of my pants.

"Here." He tucks a bottle into my hand. I uncork it and feel him piecing through my hair.

"You're a dead man," he says. I drink. "Give me your gun."

"I lost it," I tell him.

"You sold it," he says.

"No," I say. "I shot up a girl and her mother, then tossed it into the Harlem River."

"A dream. You hit your head, McGlue," he says.

We ride on through the park and up through Harlem past the pretty brick mansions and over farms and manors and up and up and I sleep, and when I wake with my head hurting Johnson gives me another bottle. I wake again in Mamaroneck with my head wrapped in gauze, the old maid chewing on her fingernail looking down at my face like a pile of dirty dishes she has to do.

"What?" I mumble.

She says nothing, and goes and puts another log on the fire.

*Lima*

I've not seen Johnson in too long. He comes and goes in my mind's eye and still he hasn't come to my lock-up down here in the boat to cool my nerves, my hot snake brains they feel like, slithering and stewing around, steam seeping through the crack in my head. I'd ask him, Johnson, to find a doctor to take my charge, since I don't know how else to get out of here.

I know I'm sick. I've been this sick before and Johnson got me better. A slow feed of whiskey, corn pone and fish pie, quick walks through the trees each noon at first and then learning day by day on a boat how to rig sails and all the knots and lugging crates and learning how to bark above the wind, sit and ride the quiet oceans. Had I liquor to spill I'd pour it directly into the crack, to cool the snakes. Get them to settle down, quit hissing. If I drink enough down my throat they lie still for a while and I can ride out a moment of my life, like I've been doing here and there. But it gets harder the longer I'm down here, the lesser Fag comes in with bottles. The ale is flat and weak. A blackie sneaks me snuff but it keeps me awake and once I spit it in the bucket I'm thirsty again. Saunders answers a question I haven't asked. "We'd got him wrapped in burlap and tied up, and he was all stiff and done bleeding, and once we were a few clicks off shore from Zanzibar we just pushed him off. But we didn't have a song or no one to make a real tribute besides Captain who said what a good man he'd been." He doesn't look my way. "So we said a prayer in our heads and dropped in a bible after him and he sunk but the bible didn't," he says. "Don't think we haven't got a heart."

"When's Johnson coming?" I ask Saunders.

He pulls the door shut again. I wait. In some time the boat stills on the water and I hear the dull and grainy sound of shore. I imagine what it looks like: Purple hills in the distance. Girls in thick red-and-white dresses, donkeys wearing carpets, bodegas full of gut-stabbing liquor. Cold wet deck I'd skip down and the gritty black dirt I'd clear bits of trash away from before I'd kiss. Lick my lips. The warm and bitter taste of solid ground. On my knees. I spit in the bucket. I call for Fag. A plate of potatoes sits on the dropped-down. I decide to stand. My feet look carbuncled and large swinging from my child-sized ankles, two soft, buoy-like calves swaying inside lengths of soiled woolen underwear. I catch my reflection in the shield-shaped mirror. It's a drawing of a hungry, long-bearded squirrel.

## Tierra del Fuego

Fag brings in great bounty, trampling news of pirates and shitting on John Bull. He's drunk and gives me a big jug of the stuff. It's called Pisco, he tells me. Nothing wrong with that.

"Made from grape wine, McGlug," he says. He's got a kind of wolfy smile on, leaning against the dropped-down, wagging his head. He trips back as the boat sways and laughs. I take a long pull on the jug. Like Scotch and wild roses, like man and woman the same, the perfect mix. I drink it down.

Fag wants more. He steps up forth and sticks his hand out. I'm cross-legged on the cot with the jug stuck at my crotch.

"Get your own," I tell him.

He reaches down.

But I push him back against the wall. I haven't pushed him hard. He kind of freezes there after his head hits, then just slides down to the floor. Faggot, I think. Drink.

When he wakes up it's night and the jug is empty and I'm sick off the side of the cot, neverminding the bucket and Fag's got his hands over his nose.

"Pig," he says to me. I can see him now crawling in the moonlight, between the shadows. It's nice. Like Johnson would be there sometimes, when I'd come to, and he'd have a smart remark to make.

"Jack-ass," he'd say. Throw a rag by my bruised and mindless hand resting on the floor. I'd wipe the puke away.

"Johnson," I croak. "How much longer til this is all over?"

"Up to you, Nick. Bottom's bottom's do or die, let the battle end and roll over."

I clear my throat, roll over.

"Good boy," I hear.

I fall to sleep.

We ride a train up from Mamaroneck and stop in New Haven and I spend a day ginning out while Johnson goes to talk to a man about jobs to no good end. Johnson finds us beds and shows me the picture he's had taken. A little brown drawing of himself in that dumb hat and satin scarf. I ask for one of my own and he seems to humor me. I like when he treats me like a child. The next day he shows me to a doctor. It's a little fat-faced doctor in a black coat near the train station and a big orange-and-yellow bird in a cage.

"She comes from Caribbio," he tells us. He whistles a note and blinks dauntedly behind his spectacles. The bird unfolds and refolds its wings.

"He fell on his head," says Johnson. "He needs a letter written in your name."

"You see me clear, sailor?" asks the doctor, waving his arms up and down.

I nod.

He holds my face in his hands and looks deep into my eyes, then peers into the crack in my head.

"You're low in spirits, looks like." I hold my breath. "One or two's okay but too many and you'll get a bottle ache. Know that?"

I nod some more.

Johnson pulls off a glove and pokes a finger between the copper wires of the birdcage. The bird takes small steps back along a little rod.

The doctor turns his back and writes.

I button up my coat.

"He may want to take a few of these if it swells up and hurts him," says the doctor. He hands Johnson a vial of tablets and the letter.

If I had that picture of Johnson I'd speak to it. I'd be with it. I'd be in it, poking at his still, so serious face, elbowing him in the ribs, saying, "Don't just stand there, say something." And then feeling a fool knowing that he'd got me again: dead play. I'd wait for him to laugh and say it: "Got you."

*Salem*

My mother isn't so happy to see me.

She comes to the door with a lit candle and a knife.

"Who's there?" she says. Her voice is ratty and grave.

"It's me," I say.

"Chicken shit."

The door swings open a crack. Her hair is greyed and buffered into the neck of her dress. She wears her big hair like a hat. I want to laugh and come inside but she just stands there. I hear her breath and it's whistley and bad. I haven't thought of her twice since I left, but there she is and I'm back.

"You can't stay here," she says. "You're dead and gone."

"Where should I go, then?" I want to know.

Johnson's at my side, and my mother sees him now and grips the door and blows the candle out. I stop the door with my foot and ask again. "Where?"

"Dwelly came by looking for you," she says. "Go ask him."

I take my foot away.

"Give me that knife," I say.

I hear her back away.

I push the door open more and keep my foot on it and grab the knife from her hand and feel her wrist, dry and pointy and like made of crinkled papers.

Back out on the road I stick the knife in my boot and we start off down the road to where I know Dwelly will be spending most of the night: the Rum Room, in back, most likely, asleep and happy.

We pass a big tree that creaks and sways and Johnson says he'd like to rest and where we are is Howard Street and I tell him we better keep on towards the wharves, where the taverns are. He wants to pack his pipe, though. He sets his back against the tree. The moonlight shakes through the leaves like a weak shaft of lightning. It's not good. I want to tell him not to lean against that tree and keep moving. "They hung a lady from that tree way back because she killed her own daughter."

He doesn't care.

"Broke her own daughter's neck. Wrung it like a chicken's. Then went around telling what she'd done to all the neighbors. Been so proud. Let's go."

"What. You from Salem still believe in witches?"

"No," I say. "But ghosts and I'm thirsty. And my brother's buried up the road."

He strikes a match and it sputters and dies before it reaches the bowl of his pipe.

"Shit." He strikes again. I get weary. My head is clear now, the night sky sparkling like wet, broken glass.

"Daughter's name was Difficult. You think it's a name for a girl you'd like?"

"I don't care what the name is, long as she gets warm."

"Guess you don't mind much," I say.

"Guess you do," he says.

He seems mad. I wonder if he'll just shove off now. Since we parted ways in New York, and since he refound me and took me over, he hasn't said much of where he's been or what he's done.

"Just fuck the world and get on, Nick," he says.

I ask him to repeat himself.

"I said, fuck the world."

It sounds all right coming out of his mouth. The word "world" rears around like something brewerful. Like something I could swallow and burp and taste and get all up in me and sick of, and I think, yeah, I'll fuck it. My head hurts suddenly. I ask Johnson for a tablet and he dumps the vial out into his palm and picks one up between his fingers and says, "Open up," and I stick my tongue out, and he sets the tablet on it—quaking, steaming tongue there, feed me, and it's bitter, and my tongue shirks and scoots and tucks back and something stills in me and something's something I don't know what and I don't care and it's good.

We retrace our path back to my mother's house and I knock again. This time when she comes to the door I've got the knife ready and I hold it out and tell her to get inside and make us two plates of food and pour the whiskey and stir the fire, because we're cold and we're hungry and I need a drink.

My mother huffs and turns and smacks her tongue but she does like I say. I laugh. I sit down inside. Johnson, chewing and yawning, barely moves his eyes from the fire. My littlest sister pokes her head in through the doorway from her bed. I cross my eyes.

"Rotten child," she says to me. "Your head looks funny."

I hold the knife up and twist it in the air and let the firelight catch the blade to scare her and watch her eyes narrow and she leaves the bottle on the table and walks slowly out of the room. Drink.

"Tomorrow," I say to Johnson, "we'll see about getting jobs."

"Mmm," says Johnson, a deep and resonant sound, and he dabs the grease from his mouth with the edge of my mother's tablecloth, his face all beset and pink and shining from the flames.

## San Juan

There's much yelling on deck I hear. Men's voices pronounce
instruction like the bleeting cries from a herd of goats to the
slaughter. None could care less if I joined in song from down here,
so I sing. I sing the first part twice and slow and full of feeling and
then the rest real quick and easy like a simple dancing tune. It goes
like this. Listen. Tell me if my voice is clear:

> *When mounted on a milk-white steed*
> *I thought myself a flash lad indeed*
> *With my cock'd pistol and broad sword*
> *"Stand and deliver" was my word*

> *The first I met was a gentleman*
> *I rode up to him and shook his hand*
> *In spite of all that he could do*
> *I took his time and kill'd him too.*

*Salem*

When I got tall enough to walk into taverns without friends' fathers
turning and huffing and wagging their thick, red and rope-burned
hands at me and pointing at the door, I took to a place called Lady
Lane's where they had a kind of bourbon called dead dog and the
barmaid was a girl named Mae and she'd let me watch her undress in
her little room in the back of the inn where she was also in charge of
making the beds and things and she kept a bottle up there and would
give it to me while I sat there and sometimes I sang a song and fell
asleep in her bed but hardly touched her. One summer night after she
quit working we went up together to her room and she unbuttoned
her dress and had me slip it off down her arms, and her arms were so
soft and warm I thought I'd be sick from how her flesh gave at the
slightest poke of my fingers, and how the thin fabric of her dress rolled
and cinched her skin and these were just her arms to start off with and
I couldn't imagine what the rest of her was going to do to me, it was
horrible, and this smell wafted up from her bosom like sour milk and
like the foul rank from the docks almost, and I gagged and she was
sort of shaking and breathing towards me like a fat, stupid child after
running, and she looked at me and asked in a soft and malmsey voice
was I all right and her eyes looked so big and wet but I knew that what
she meant to ask was was I some kind of scared little puppy and was I a
baby who'd never been with a woman's arms before and all that, and so
I pushed her down and her hair sort of flew up around her face like she

was underwater and she fell on her knees and grinned and squinted her eyes and turned her back to me and started to kind of crawl like a cat towards the bed. It wasn't good.

So I just took her by the arm and tied her to the wooden rail of her balcony and took her keys and went back down to the empty tavern and drank more dog till the sun rose and then went back home and forgot about the girl.

At Lady Lane's the next night the big man in charge was there with his face red and whispering loudly and steamily at the girl which was not unusual and the girl came up to me and said through grit teeth, "Bully for you, you faggot bum," and I just pushed my cup aside and tapped the table the way a man does to mean he wants more to drink. This I remember.

When we reach the wharf on the waterfront in Salem Seaport I'm told to dress and gather my things. Then Saunders comes in and hands me a bottle and shakes my hand and steps out and leaves the door open and Fag is there in the doorway waiting. I throw the blankets back and take a look at my sea legs. Barely have I walked away from this bed in months. I stand slowly with the bottle weighing me down on one side and lurch to where Saunders has put a pile of clothes and a pair of shoes on top. I take a swig and dress with one hand and hold the bottle in the other. My old clothes are all too big. Without a belt I must hold my trousers up with my free hand. Fag watches with his head down, thumbs his lip impatiently, looks forlorn.

My mother's standing down by the docks with my youngest sister, a man at her side holding her arm. I barely feel my feet hit the ground when they do. Most men are busy unrigging and unloading and I understand that I'm to go with the constable and his men with their shiny brass badges now gleaming under the cloudy sky, the trees, the heights of things and the stillness and the way I move towards the world, the skin of my mother's face so pale it's nearly purple, the man's chin hairs wavering softly. I look around for Johnson. They take me to a cart with bars over the windows and I get in and Fag is gone now. I open my mouth to speak and my ears hurt and I can hear again. It sounds like wind. The policeman shuts the door and says nothing. I'm thirsty, I'd like him to know. The air hurts my head. It's quiet. The ground moves eventually and I sit in the darkened splintery box-cart. My bones bump. Johnson reads from the *Daily Atlas*:

*Capt. Isaac Hedge, well known in New Bedford and Salem as shipmaster from those ports, and formerly of Barnstable, committed suicide on the passage from San Francisco to Panama, by first cutting his throat and then jumping overboard.*

"I never knew him," I say.

*Mad dogs have been terrorizing New Bedford.*

I hear him flip the page.

There was a time I knew there was a god hearing my thoughts and I was careful what I let get said and there was a time the shame of what I heard up there made me bang my head against the wall and then I grew tall enough to walk into Lady Lane's and stuff my ears with liquor. That must be where they're taking us: Lady Lane's. After so long at sea. God bless them, bump, bump. Let's let the past rest in peace, hey, Johnson. Sorry, sorry. Let me buy you a bottle. Think of how far we've come.

*Howard Street*

I'm in Howard Street, I take it. I've got one window. I'm in now. Striped suit and all of it. Inmate. In trouble. In for it. I've arrived.

I haven't had a drink since the morning. They took away my things and made me bathe, measured me, wrote my name in a book. The suit they've given me to wear is a second-hand one, well-worn and patched, black-and-white and greyed and begrimed with what feels like sorriness. I'm not sorry, though. Better here than down in that hold, thank God. These are like proper pajamas. Made of soft cotton. I won't complain. Though I wonder when my mother will come with a package, if they'll ask me for a list of what I'll need for the night. They better. Here's my homecoming.

The guard through the iron bars is an oversized fellow with a young face but no hair. Looks like Dwelly Pepper's big brother but I don't mention that since I know it's not him. He tells me something in the gnarlmouth way of the Irish. Bet he drinks. He yaps a bit without looking in on me and I don't understand though I feel like we know each other. He sits on a peg-legged wooden stool and stands when somebody walks by, lifts one haunch to blow a fart from time to time. He's okay. I watch him pick his nose and rub his head. I rub my head. I try to joggle something up there with the butt of my hand, banging at the crack, trying different angles. There's a spot in my brain caught in free-fall, from when I fell from the train, but I cannot get to it. I persist, though. I think if I get past a certain point in the skull I can push down on the place that was so good. I feel I'm making progress when a soft spot tenderizes beneath the pressure of my thumb, like the breakdown of gristle. Then my ears stop working, which is one advancement, I think, first off. But it's just that I can't hear what's outside of me. Everything inside is perfectly clear: all the cringey nerves and blood, swimming vessels puckered and empty and breath blowing for nothing and bones just creaking, mad, swaying like strained and knotted rope, like my shoulders, my jaw, all held in place so tight they're about to snap. My stomach growls. I watch the guard. He seems not to mind me slapping myself up like this. He seems loose, like I doubt there's much I could do to baffle him. I wonder what in his life he's seen. I grip my throat with my hands and strangle for a minute then get tired, play dead. He just chews on his nails, all hunkered over himself, elbows on knees, spitting skillfully at the floor.

It's good to feel tired and just lie and look around.

I've got a pot to shit and piss in again. There's a jar of water and a tin cup on a little table and the ground is still. I could be happy here, I think, depending on a steady supply. But I worry. Where is it?

Then like some loud noise of a sudden I am in it bad again. Nothing ever seemed so impossible as to have to spend the day like this, between the walls like this here. To be anywhere but here, or what I wouldn't give for just one sip, or to have someone else in here with me at the very least, just anything but not to have to be here, sitting, lying down with myself like this. Not going anywhere. The walls are made of flat-cut, grainy grey stone blocks.

I close my eyes, but because the sun is pouring in so bad through the window I need to squinch my eyes up and cover my face with my hands to make it disappear and get it so I'm on the ship again and Johnson and me are feeding rope side by side, steadying the shrouds, then putting on the ratlines, and the ship rocks us and I feel my innards sway and rise and I sweat and hear mates yelling and I hold up a hand to keep the sun from my eyes and I'm blind and others run up thundering and I hear Johnson's voice afar now and catch the whiff of another unwashed man hanging in the salt air, wind still for a moment as the ship turns, a cold bare spot of my skin—just the back of my hand—scratched by the bristly husk of hair on his arm, feel the heat of that body, let it warm me. Like whiskey to the heart it lets me know who I am and where I'm going and the answer is it doesn't matter at all, it's nothing, it's empty air and just right and the wind picks up and we're on, fast, sun behind us, everywhere. I lower my hands and the mates stand and breathe. I'm at rest for a moment. Screw Johnson, the shit, I don't care. The ground is still. So I open my eyes. I'm in jail.

A tray of bread and beans is slid through a space in the barred door. Barefooting across the floor I see the guard has a newspaper on his lap. He lifts his face at me then sets it back down. The food looks not so bad. I hold the bread in my hand and squeeze. It smells sharply of yeast, the beans of lard. I call out to the guard. "What's news?" He doesn't hear me. I stand. I feel not so clear, I feel tired. The floor and ceiling switch places and the earth quakes. A moment later the guard comes down across my face fist-first: "Shut it!" he shouts into my ear. I quit screaming. I've been screaming.

"Oh," I say. "Oh, all right," I tell the guard. "Thank you."

With that punch I've been straightened out. The guard picks me up and drags me to the bed. Straw from the mattress sticks up and riles me, all poke and scratchy. I swallow some blood, a tooth. It feels good. My ears ring bright with song from like getting boxed. The day feels over. I'm happy. I want to know his name, this fellow, my guard. I try to speak but my mouth just gurgles. I laugh through my nose. I hear him huffing and then footsteps.

Out the window snow is falling and it's pretty. If I wrench my neck completely I can see the bare-branch tops of trees that line the commons where I used to play ball, the violet sky. It reminds me. When there was no liquor left at home and Dwelly's dad and Rich's dad were keeping them home and my mom had her purse on her and was out somewhere, I had a nice roster of other things that worked. Like bending over and putting my head in a pillowsack. Or hanging my feet from the rafters and getting little sister to press my throat with the old leather strap used for horses. Hit my head against the floor. A gulp of blood is one good substitute. It was Johnson's tastes like rum. Mine's more like soured wine. I listen to my ears ring and watch the snow.

Where there would be sleep that night there is very simply no sleep.

The guard now is a fat greybeard and has moved his stool down the hallway. I see a small candleflame on a windowsill down that way, its light twisted in the glass. Shadows move strange and soft with the slow light, the shifting snow reflecting wind in trails of lights and darks along the walls, the brightened sky, the creeping growth of frost on the window.

I think to throw my cup against the bars and demand a blanket. But I'm too cold to move. Anyway I don't think I should have to ask. My breath is smoke in the air and just visible in the dim light here in my cell. I do miss my old cot. Fag. Here all I've had is my emptied jar dunked in a bucket of water dragged down the hall by a man with red hair. That and the water tastes of rotted egg. All this to-do at a sickened sailor. They may think if they quarantine me and whatever is my disease then I'll do no harm to the people here. I've heard it done before when men come home with the flux or a case of pox or whatnot—just left in confines like this. Seems punishment enough to be so sick. It's not good here, no.

I wrap myself in the one sheet, cover my feet with the bottom lengths of my pants, shiver hard, head wobbling off my neck like dolls we saw in the market stalls in China. And somehow I sweat. And the drops of sweat from my shaking brow fall and freeze and collect in the creases of my clothes, snow, and it seems right that somebody ought to give us a drink to put us to bed about now, since I am a guest in their service, aren't I, and so I sit here, huffing and blowing smoke and snowing, expectant of an orderly or nurse or blackie with a bottle on a tray. I'll hold my cup out. They ought to be coming soon, since the lights are out. My mouth has in it the dry, tinny taste of dirt. My lips are bumpy and taste still of salt air, the sea. I think I hear footfalls and I take a deep breath and hold it and listen. But it's quiet and no one is coming. When I let my breath out the smoke takes a shape. Looks like a man sitting off to one side at the foot of the bed.

I'm too cold to talk to him, and I barely lift my head so as not to disturb the cavity of heat held down around me by the sheet. But I keep my eyes on the smokeman. He's drinking a bottle. He takes his hat off and fits it on his knee. Looks as though he's waiting for something. Has the posture of a happy drunk. My age.

I clear my throat to see if he'll turn my way.

He just takes another swig and stares at the floor, then cranes his neck wide like looking off into a distance. But then he says, "Your guy will be along, Mick."

It's Dwelly Pepper's voice.

"You ought to set things right," he says, fingering his hat now. "People say you two had some kind of scrap out there and you made off the better somehow. Don't know how you did it but you ought to fix it, I think."

"What did you hear, Dwelly?" I want to know.

"Heard there was a scrap between you. You and him. At the last leg or what and didn't tell anyone what it was for. And before that you'd asked for leave somewhere. What was that about?"

"China."

"What for?"

"Captain should have let me stay. I was just asking for the money owed me. There was a beach town in the south there, kind of away from things. I could have just stayed. It seemed like a good idea."

"Seems like the worst idea I ever heard."

"You wouldn't get it, Dwelly."

"You sound all grum, McGlue. What's with that?"

"I'm sick, I think."

"But you sound more than sick," Dwelly says, leaning closer.

I look down into my lap, breathe the warmer air trapped in there under the sheet. I think Dwelly will go away if I stay like this.

"Do tell," Dwelly says.

"I'd rather not."

"Well, all right."

"Give me that bottle, Dwelly."

"You know I won't."

"Is Johnson coming at all?"

"Don't get too puckered out, now. He'll be here."

I duck my head out and breathe some more smoke into Dwelly.

"Dwelly," I tell him. "My head hurts."

"I don't doubt it," Dwelly says, and lifts the bottle and raps it down on my skull just where my crack is. "And how now, Mick?"

"Better."

A shadow noiselessly walks up along the floor.

"Say something," Dwelly says, pointing at it.

"Johnson?"

It's him.

I wish Dwelly would go away.

Johnson's just standing there, waiting, grey and still by the bed, bent up on the wall. He says nothing. I try to make a gesture with my eyes, to let him know I want to talk, but not in front of Dwelly.

"What are you waiting for?" Dwelly says. "Tell him you're sorry and all that."

I roll my eyes.

"Give me the rest of what's in that bottle, Dwelly," I say.

He raps me on the head again.

Johnson just stays there. Like he's saying, "I'm here." Like he's saying, "I'm all yours now," or something.

My breath is white and Dwelly.

"It'll be warmer in the day. We'll talk then, alone," I say.

"You all bitches," says Dwelly. "Always with keep-away, God."

It makes some sense, though I know I'm dreaming.

I just lay down, cold as it is, until Dwelly disappears. Finally, I feel sleep.

The doctor is sent in to see me. It's morning. I still shiver.

He hands his coat and hat to the day guard and rubs his hands together. Glimmer on his satin vest hurts my eyes.

"Be quiet," he says, before I open my mouth. He looks into my eyes and sniffs my breath, makes no expression. His skin is thick, tanned and oiled, beard patched on the sides of his face kind of mangy.

"How much longer?" I try to ask.

"Hush," he says. His voice is not unkind. I look at him some more. He's looking at me, fingering my jaw, my hair, my ankles, lifting my knees, then straightening them and turning me on my belly and lifting my shirt. It's too cold to hold still so I jerk and twist and stutter. He pokes a finger at some spots on my backside.

"It hurts?" he asks.

It does, but I jiggle my head no.

"A drink would alleviate the head is all," I manage. He ignores it.

Another man comes with a piece of paper. The doctor gets up to tell him something. A vial of pills appears. I sigh.

"These are vitamins," he says, hair drifting off his brow as he bends over to look me in the eye. "You'll take them every day when you eat. And no more liquor. You'll be dead soon with it, no question. And your head won't heal as long as you keep bashing it against the floor. All right then."

He pats my shoulder with just the tips of his fingers and goes. The policeman who took me from the boat yesterday meets him in the hall and shakes his hand.

"You're black-and-blue heres," says the guard, pointing at his lower back, then at mine. His face looks like a child's, seen something he can't believe. He leaves and gives the doctor his coat and hat and locks the bars again.

I'd say my cell was six feet wide, ten feet long and ten high last night, and this morning it's four feet wide, eight feet long and seven feet high.

Afternoon. I've been standing up in front of the window, smearing my nose along a stripe of sleeve, wondering if anyone from the road would look up to see me if I started screaming and pounding the glass, and if they did would they point and wave, or do what, I wonder. They brought me my food this morning and I ate it all. Haven't put any shit in the bucket yet. Took two pills from a pale pig-nosed guard with water. Bitter taste did nothing for me. Sat back down full-bellied and could have died. Perhaps this is sorrow. This is what they mean.

An old man is standing outside the gate. He's squinting and giving me the up and down, nodding constantly.

"Smaller than I expected," he says.

He leans back and nudges the guard who gets up to let him into my cell. I just stand there.

"I've been hired by your mother. Chosen to represent you. As counsel. I can't tell you she had much choice in the matter as I may be the only litigator in the region without any loyalties to this family of Johnsons, the father being William Johnson who as I'd guess you know had quite a stake in this town since Naumkeag Steam along with the other higher ups—not my neighbors, look at me—and so has much of the common people here—my neighbors, your neighbors, or your mother's neighbors more like—under pressure or at least the ones that need jobs and will have them now that half the state's gone off in pursuit of dreams of gold and sunshine, those idiots. I told my nephew the cure to unhappiness isn't to go run off to some dumb fantasy but you know these young men, get something in their head and can't get it out till it's nearly killed them, and even I remember that and how I would not be discouraged by any old man, and I thought twenty-five was old, you know. I remember looking up at my cousin Roddy, ha, that mule, thinking 'One day I'll have money to buy myself a hat like that,'

thinking he was so proud, could do anything he wanted. But we're
limited, aren't we? We've all got some limitations. And we bump up
against them, and it hurts, sure, but it's the only way to find them out.
Hmm. I hear you've done some damage up there." He points to my
head. So far he's been shuffling papers from his worn leather satchel
and taking out a pen and ink and then removing his coat and putting
it back on and arranging himself on the foot of the bed. He stops now,
though, and gets up and comes towards me, eyes set on my crown, and
just sort of sniffs, blows my hair with his lips in a whistle.

"That looks bad. That looks very bad." He nods some more. "Good.
If we can pin this all on the dead brains and get that doctor to attest
to what madness you've been brewing up there, that's nice, very nice.
A jury is well-swayed by a sick man, pity's good. And a doctor's word
is barely gotten the gist of, so we make claims to something very
complicated. If all fails, and I hope we won't have to bring this up, and
you can be plain with me, sailor, I've been alive long enough to know
it takes all kinds, we'll touch on what it was between you and Johnson,
just what it really was, without recalling whatever details—and you
don't need to be that precise with me, of course—so as not to solicit
additional charges, since that would not be good. And know this about
me. I don't judge. We are all children of God, aren't we, etcetera." He
waits for my eyes to meet his.

"What?" I say.

"Yes, yes, all right. Shake hands." He stands before me and sticks
out his hand. I uncross my arms. My hand shakes on its own. He grabs it.

"I'm Foster. Cy."

"Sigh."

"That's it."

I think to ask him to bring me a bottle. He's all kind of old and rascally and like maybe not smart enough to know when he's being pawned. I wonder what sort of compensation he's gathering from my mom. He turns and goes to the corner of the cell where the little table is and lifts the water jug and cup and places them carefully on the floor. He drags the table towards the bed and sits at it.

"Come let's get started," he says, and pats a spot on the bed beside him. I go and sit. I think of where to rest my hands. He pulls his spectacles from his breast pocket and starts to make a pile of papers and talks again.

"You do read, don't you?"

"Yeah, I read."

He points to a drawing of a shirtless, bearded madman on a wooden dock with jungle trees and monkeys behind him. The madman holds a wide rig knife in a posture of apemanship—legs bent and splayed, head sunk forward. Another man is drawn lying belly-up on the dock, dressed in a straight-lined suit and tall hat. Strokes like heat, or greatness, rise from his body. A naked black tribesman holds a tall blade-tipped shaft and covers himself with a sign that reads: NOT FOR SALE.

"I don't get it," I tell the lawyer. Foster.

"Republicans. Never mind. But you can see already everyone thinks you're crazy."

"That's me?" The shirtless, bearded ape.

"What they'd like to think of you, yes—some animal with no manners, and stink. But I don't see that here. You're barely a pigeon. Not much to you. You should eat more."

"I will."

"They feed you?"

"Only food."

We are quiet.

"I need your signature on a few of these."

He hands me the pen and points. I make a puddle of my name on one, and scratch something on the other. Foster holds my wrist for the third.

"I need to know frankly what happened."

He is looking at me as though I will tell him. He has the pen between his fingers, mouth agape slightly, listening to me breathe. I have no intention of speaking until my head gets straight. I have nothing to say. I look at the old man and widen my eyes, sort of. I mean to tell him to let me rot and die, just bring me whiskey, wine, anything. He reads my expression like I'm asking to be comforted. Or something.

"It'll get better," he says. "Keep your mind moving. Time goes faster when you're busy. It probably will save your life, this incarceration. I'd take that very seriously if I were you. No more poison, and you've got to come clean with me so I can defend you. Decide now, my boy. If I'm going to work to get you out just to die, well, don't waste my time is all. Maybe you were provoked. I need to know. I'll be back in a few days." And he takes his papers and goes.

But he leaves the newspaper, dated yesterday.

I sit at the table and watch the floor for Johnson. It's warmer, but my head and hands still shake. The front page of the paper has got one column that's called "Counting Room Almanac for 1851" and all it is is a calendar of the year, each month and all the numbered days, from yesterday till the end. That's how much longer I have, it's like.

I pick up the paper and unfold it. Inside is a knife. I hide it in the mattress and sit down to read.

The paper is very useful.

The world of Dry Goods is luxury: doeskins, vestings, all wool tweeds. Colored cambrics, printed cashmeres and fancy Earlston ginghams. Velvets. All that soft wadding. I imagine it's Johnson's natural habitat, a cradle filled with fluffy silk pillows. He sought out these rank and fuck-it muddy pastures, the shit I showed him. He was just a student of misery. He had this idea that there was something like grace and victory to be found in smiting your good fortune, choosing the worst. In answering what he would do with his life say to follow the most putrid path, to ruin his life. See, he was all kind and mete when I met him that night in the snow. By Spain he wasn't impressed by anything. Spat on whores in Seville and thought himself worldly, that moron. And later shed tears on the ship to me, speaking what I thought at the time were really heartwrung philosophies. Life words. And I awoke for him, always, to listen. To me it felt like more than conversation. But I don't think he ever had much respect. I was like a heavy bleached cottonade that would hold a lot and show much of what he let spill. A vanity. But by that time I was already drunk on him. And I told him how it felt to wear the cloak of his shit. It felt good, I said. It felt better than drunk, I'd tell him. He said he knew what I meant. He'd cry, do you understand what I'm saying? It was black serge and grey and pale pink silk scarves like that, near like that, alone together squatted down out of the wind, in the mud, drunk and tired and unwatched and me with my head on my knees and Johnson's hands in my hair, warm and near and together like that like bridge and tide and roof and blinded by sunlight and swaddled, me swaddled in love for him like a wolf in blankets like fine grey merinos, drunk as brothers. Like pale brown satinets. Like royal blue flannel and orleans, alpaca blankets.

Otherwise I feel at home in MERCHANDIZE: white beans, fleece and corn. Simply put, without Johnson I'm just mess pork, sugar, tallow oil, cannel coal and rye. And always Superior Irish Whiskey, ten casks, just received via Rio Grande, for sale by Russel & Tilson. A bed, a window, floor, walls and little table. The ink from the paper turns my hands grey. Like shadow rubbing off on me. "The Concert on Christmas Evening" lifted backwardedly off across my wrist.


The next morning Foster arrives with a package.

"You're still here," he says. "From the church." He puts the brown-paper wrapped thing down on the bed.

I'm with the newspaper, seated on the floor with my back against the wall. I find it the most comfortable and the least drafty place, here in the corner.

"Some kind of ruckus outside at the docks to do with a ship leaving to a big show in London. The whole town was gathered to see them load this big machine, looked like a reaper or some huge iron trap, my God. I asked a young kid up front what it was for and he said it's for making shoes. Have you ever heard such a thing? People will line up for any kind of disaster of logic, I swear. And these are the people who will sit in judgment when your time comes, you know. Are they smart or are they stupid? We don't care. They like a good story, though. And they want to be right. They want very badly to be right. Do you know what I mean?" he asks me.

I'm looking up at him. I hear what he's saying. I feel very bad. I think to tell him, "I'm not well down here. The air isn't right. I may use the knife," but he's so expectant and alive there, now sitting with his legs crossed, deeply denting the bed, I don't think he'll let me be. He will want me to explain myself. Better to just nod and oblige him. He is my lawyer. He looks at his shoes and points.

"All that for this. Unbelievable."

"Unbelievable," I repeat.

He eyes me warily, as though mocked, then turns and prepares his pen and paper.

"Wait a moment." He goes to the gated door and pulls a bell from his pocket. The sound reminds me of schooldays and my teacher and the smooth black slate which I wrote my name on. The girls with ribbons in their hair. Boys. Ruddy-cheeked, emblazoned with freckles, blue and green and brown eyes open, toothy and lazy-headed, light from the window, poke me on the shoulder, say, "Hey, want to fly my kite after?" Then go have lunch and not come back. Run down the muddy river path and go swimming if it was warm.

Nobody cared where I was then. Foster comes back with a little stool and puts it on the other side of the little table.

"Now we have a proper office, eh." He sits on the stool.

"Come," he says. From his coat pocket he pulls a small paper bag of sweets. "Take one, please. Go on."

I put one in my mouth and sit.

"They're lemon, yes?"

I nod.

"Well, all right," he begins. "To start off let's know that the people of this place don't have a soft record when it comes to convicting people of evildoing. The poor souls. You know, don't you, that in the early years if you were the least bit own-minded they'd call you a devil and burn you like a pig, roast you. There was nothing like a defense lawyer for someone they called a witch, nobody to prove them wrong by law. The law was all set up to keep people convinced their fears were well-guided. They came up with ways to prove themselves right about people who seemed a little different. All witches, they said, felt pain if you stuck them in the ribs and sank in water if you tied them down. For God's sake, of course. Now we know it's what's called a personality—a difference of opinion. And thank God for that freedom, right, right. And these children pretending spells and things. All just spoiled brats dipping their hands in the wrong pots, I think. You seen someone with the Danbury shakes? What do you call it—hatmakers' disease? Solvents for the furs make you dance like a wild rabbit. Things get into your brain. Well, you know. Things have made their way into your brain, to be sure. Who knows? What's done is done, anyway. I don't believe in

evil, I'll let you know. I think the Devil's just a story to scare children
so they act right. And I think we should have more respect than
to scare one another straight. I think people act in error, sure. It's
human. God alone is perfect and the rest is for shit, excuse me. So
who's to blame? That's why I'm on the defensive side. It's a natural
fit with me. Not anyone should be condemned. Are you all right?
You look very pale."

"I'm all right," I say.

"The church people, the women from my wife's church, our
church, my wife's churchlady friends, have knitted you this blanket."

Foster rips the paper with the sharp nail of his pinky.

"I think this blanket will become like a balm. You ever had
something like that? A blanket that was like a balm?"

"What do you mean by balm?" I ask. I am already bored. I take
another candy. It's good. He tosses the blanket across the bed.

"Like a blessed thing that soothes, a balm." He pauses. "Tell me
about this Johnson. What your rapport was like. What this rivalry
was about at the end, which led you to kill him. That I need to
know."

I chew the candy and pull the blanket across my lap.

"In so many words," he says, "there was some kind of
disagreement. Is that right?"

"There had been, yeah."

"And the disagreement had to do with what, would you say?"

"It had to do with what Johnson wanted."

"And what was that."

"He wanted to die, I can only guess."

✤

My mother comes the next day waving a sheath of papers. She starts in yelling, pausing every now and then to shield her face and eye me as though she expects I'll make a run for her.

"Do you know they made me lift my skirt before unlocking that first iron door, hey? A grown woman. As though I'd have snakes and daggers and bloody hell up there? All kinds of trouble, my boy, since you showed up again. I swear. Rocks through my window and Sissy's got a black eye from some kids at the park. What all this is I can't believe, my God. And this."

She smoothes the papers down on the little table, bends over, huffing. Her hair is pulled tight back like I've never seen it. Like she'd taken off the top part of her head, no poof. We are face-to-face now.

"My God, baby," she says, "what happened to all your teeth?"

I look down at the papers. It's Johnson's writing.

"This letter," she starts, "got to me yesterday by one of the young kids off some ship."

I begin to read it.

"Well, what's it say?" she asks, spitting over my shoulder. "That's your name there, isn't it? He says you owe him money or something, is that it?"

I roll my eyes and throw my head back. I see all white for a few moments.

"Hello? Hello?" my mother says. "You do break my heart, you know." She pets my head, smoothing the hair down, careful not to touch the crack.

I protest and hear my voice like a little boy's. She's pulling the churchblanket up to my shoulders, folding it under my armpits, saying "shhh."

"Next time bring a few bottles. They don't have anything to drink here."

She's petting my head and starts to cry.

"Just they give me these hard pills I choke on, it hurts, mom."

"I'll talk to them."

"No, just bring it, okay?"

"I'll see what I can do."

"Do what I say."

"Shh."

I sit up in bed and take her hand hard.

"Next time have two bottles. Or else I won't see you."

She tries to do something like to soothe me but it's like daggers in my eyes and I get her with both hands and twist one arm behind and yeah, so I see what it is has been holding her hair back and it's like a wooden fork all twisted like rope around a tee so I just yank it and here it comes, a big wave of grey bushelling over her shoulders, my mother yelping, "Let me go, you bastard."

Then "Guard?" she yells. "You are sick. Poor boy. 'That's just his manner,' is what I told that lawyer. He said I'd been a drunk's fool, I nearly spat. A mother's love is so dumb."

The guard comes and lets her out. I stuff the papers under the mattress. I hold the blanket over my head, just wrap it around my head and breathe hard until I'm too tired to hold on. I sleep.

+

Things Johnson's said that come back to me now:

"Nobody knows how cruel I'd like to be."

"Let them clean it up."

We were out drinking one afternoon the week before our ship left port, sitting up on the wooden bridge over the inlet where the railroad ran by, hanging our legs off, just looking down. It was going to rain. Johnson said he was going to go home and rip his father's heart out. I asked him what he meant. He said he was going to go back to his father's house, find him, rip his father's chest open with his bare hands, then tear his heart out with his teeth.

We kept drinking for a while.

"Let's go for a steak, McGlue," he said when it started to rain.

We walked a while up Federal Street, and at the big white house before North we stopped and Johnson goes up the front walk and doesn't say anything to me but hops the steps to the door and knocks with his fist. This fat old lady answers the door and Johnson walks right in past her and leaves me out on the road. I just keep walking and go down Front and to the Rum Room and get under a table quick with Dwelly. I don't know what he's saying but there's chickens in there. Some young girl dancing, then her father comes to throw her in the mud. All these new Irish. On and on. Eventually Johnson shows up, all dry and wearing a new jacket and buys a bottle and whistles for me to come. We drink it in a carriage and go down to this big fancy place. That Hathorne from the customs house sat at the next table with the

mayor, chewing something looked like someone's pinky finger. Two
steaks came, and a cut glass bottle of brandy, I think. I was still
wearing my hat, put some silver in my pockets. Johnson chewed
his steak. Mine was on the plate, still bleeding. Candlelights from
chandeliers swinging from the ceiling. We were like on a sinking
ship. Fires alit and got put out soon as I reeled my head around. The
chime and rustle of men in stuffed chairs and their tablemanners,
voices somehow contained beneath the low music, a young pale boy
playing songs on a piano. I cut my steak with the knife provided,
held it down with the two-pronged fork. The big pieces got chewed
and swallowed. Wine came. A thin man draped my lap in white
linen over and over. Johnson was talking, I don't know what. I leaned
to the side at some point and regurgitated the entire evening. I
looked down and waited for the steam to clear. Like a breathy lizard
under the table, that. There was a red ruby ducking down below the
surface of the pile of vomit. I stuck my hand in to grab it. No luck. I
tried again. Someone handed Johnson a cigar and a monkey came to
light it with a match. I drank a gin cocktail and felt better. I began
to sing a song.

"Quiet, Mick," says Johnson handing me a wad of bills across
the table. "Keep it," he says, "but first slit my throat."

This I can remember.

## Howard Street

Before I am dressed in proper pants and jacket, my hair is cut and I'm
given a pen, ink and paper to write my confession for the judge.

"Write whatever you remember from beginning to end," my lawyer
tells me. His verbosity has been shortened the longer I've shoved him
off. "You're a quiet little wolf," he's said. I detect I've put some stink
in his brain, if just by proximity from mine. He says maneuvering a
pen around will help to revive my mind, which I can't say I doubt. But
I just hold the newspaper on my lap most mornings, read of cargo,
the price of spices, China and the visions of its new black-whiskered,
self-proclaimed Christ. And what else? The president says not to treat
men like mules. I like that. I like to see the date printed. I hold the
newspaper up to the lit window. That's the world there, I think: printed
news inside those crackling windowframes. The president says up here,
northerly, I am short-shrifted, wrongfully blamed and wrongfully
ruded. I think I'll show my lawyer. The blank paper he's given me curls
and drifts in the draft across the table. "Whatever you remember" is
hard to find. I remember my happier times from when I was a kid, fine,
but that's not what's being asked. The newspaper crinkles and speaks in
sounds beneath my fidgeting fingers. I look again.

*May we always look back with pleasure upon the past. May its
experience prove a guide for the future.*

In truth it is a miracle I can read at all, my head broken as it is and
my mind constantly on what is not going down my throat. But I should

say that my vision of a drink is less potion than pain as I see it these days. I'd rather not think of it at all. Something has altered beneath the few still live wires on the surface of my brain. I am beginning to be thirsty for something more. I can barely explain it. And I feel I don't know anything. I never did, as a kid or man, nothing. I always refused to learn.

As a kid I paid no mind to teacher in school. We were, Dwelly especially and me, always more prone to fights in the schoolyard. We preferred to knock down some old man on the road, steal and play games than that tisket-and-tasket nonsense the teacher would have us do. I had no mind for that arithmetic. What could she do anyway? We'd push her down in the mud if she was one of the young ones and take the afternoon to throw rocks down at people walking by in the park from up in trees. Small rocks, pebbles warmed up in our hands until that right time someone just so smart came by. And there were rules back then. Success and failure weighed heavy in the same area. If we missed we had to jump down from the tree to get more rocks then climb back up again. If we hit we jumped down also, but ran. I was quick and light and flew through the air like a spright bird. Dwelly, though, was fat and went slow and all bouncy and I laughed and called him names. But there were other boys without the fat-lipped bounce of Dwelly. Jack Malcolm had hands like grit rock, always clenched, hair thick and birds-nested, some kind of shadow moving behind his eyes, I thought. And Torrence who always lied and stole then cried and hit his head on the walls—something I grew to love from him. He scraped his face along the sharp brick then skulked home like a beat cat. And then later, finally, there was Johnson. These have been my only friends.

It is true my memory has suffered a long time from my love for grog. More than once I've woken up at Johnson's side with no remembrance of myself or hisself and what had brought me there, anywhere, how I'd come to live at all really. And Johnson so quiet, never saying, though I know beneath the still, warm-cheeked face of sleep were the sting and punch of what was there just as close as it was far away—me and what I had to offer him. He liked me because I was all cold, something he could never be. He called me stiff by day, dead in the face, hard to read. When I drank, I said more, showed more. But I could never meet him where he was—he never drank as much as I did. He got sick if he tried. Instead he swayed, excited, and got dull to talk with. With lavish fervor he went on about expensive things— futures, twinkling lights, music, some vision, some idea. He would go on and on about his lot without much to let me in on what he ever meant, really. "Give me another," was what I mostly said to him at these moments, and he paid. I remember the knife he carried at his back looked expensive—mother-of-pearl handle and so clean at the blade, I don't think he'd ever used it. He made my eyes roll, but I cared for him, of course, best I could. His hips swung like a narrow dog's when he walked. This I remember.

Foster taps his soft finger on the paper and looks at me closely. "How do you feel?" he asks.

Fatherly face and all, I still don't trust him. He speaks too often of the church, his old lady, how he's come to realize such-and-such. I stop listening.

"What you cannot do let God do," he tells me. "If you start writing, it will come. The real story is up in there, have faith."

"If anything even happened on whatever night you mean, I was too drunk to give it any attention," I say.

"Nothing goes unremembered. You were there. We have every reason to believe you are the one who killed him."

That is when my heart feels tight. I picture walking next to Johnson, shadow of death on his side, and my side full of briny sunshine. Doesn't he know I prefer the dark, which my eyes are so accustomed to? There is no reason to it. The one who killed him had it all wrong.

"Fine," I tell the old man, and put the pen to paper. "I was born," I write. But I can't remember what went on before I could say things in my head and hear them and hold them in myself, and maybe I was five years old then, or eight when I really woke up that way. I remember days at home, my mother. I had a brother then, one that was more than me and brave and cooked at the fire and pushed me away when I put my hand out for it. I won't remember his name now. I remember we had a little cat, and it chased the mice and my brother was the one to pick them up dead, just plain in the fist, and throw them down at the gutter for the dogs. He had brittle blue eyes like a tired pastor. He talked to me nights in bed of whatever high stakes plans he'd built up during the day, his dreams, his visions, girls he thought were pretty. The cat loved him. It purred and pranced towards him like a squirrel, scurrying around his ankles wherever he went. I was just weasling in and out of school and home then, no plans or visions besides me haunting up more trouble. I was maybe half the size of the man I am. I had the idea I wouldn't get any bigger and was mad. I put the pen down.

They say in the paper that this Chinaman Christ is going to take over the world. They are always saying these things. The people here, in this town, county, see what looks bad and make it worse. They'll twist your nose until it smells death in a bed of roses. This Christ says he's seen the face of God. You'd think they'd set him on a throne, the world, not curse him in the papers for being a scourge. A scourge is what they must call me too, I'm sure. Who have I hurt besides myself, I'd like to yell out the window. They'll say Johnson. My mother will come with crossed arms. And the churchmen and women will force my head back and try to get what's inside of it out. They'll poke at the hole in my skull while my eyes roll back, a sickly drip of what they think is evil rolling down my neck and into a bucket on the floor beneath me. I can see it. The only way to heaven, they'll tell me, those witches.

"All wrong." This is what the ladies from the church said when they stood in our house. I am a boy and my mother is in a chair scooted in at the table too tight for her arms to do anything but lay across the long-cracking wood. It's back when our home was a little room on the back face of the mill, a little house in between other little houses all the same where the women worked and the children played in the rocks and mucked around the canal. I see it, these ladies from the church coming with a tied-up package of a new pot and fresh rags and sack of flour for my mother, as though more rags is just what my mother needs. They bustle around the small home, batting at dust, lifting the curtains off the two small windows as though shocked and disgusted by the darkness, then once seeing the view of the back road through the thick, warbled glass, they set the curtains down again and wipe their hands on their big skirts. They are dressed in parched black dresses and have faces like the drippings of a candle. To me they are witches. They sneer and taunt, holding up a finger smidged with dust. My shameful mother picks at the crumbs stuck inside a crack in the table with a knife.

Children and God, these ladies are saying. I've been chewing at licorice and watching. My brother is standing with his arms crossed at the door. He has a mean look in his eye. The women open a cupboard and laugh. My brother goes and shuts it. Then my mother is saying something and crying.

It was a stenchy, grittled place, that house. Things were always falling down, and water was always coming up through the floor. When we left for church with those ladies, my brother stayed behind. They were building something between the canal and the mill, some kind of new wall. They were banging something down, I remember. We went to the church, my mother told me, because she wanted to change. She didn't want to raise us in a house of filth anymore. It was showing up, she said, on my face.

No lie, it felt good sitting there on the bench beside my mother, her hand on mine, watching the chorus sing. Above the altar a wooden man hung magically bleeding, his head bowed and face hurt but not unhappy. That was God, they told me. But I knew that wasn't God. I had the feeling, like alone on the road at night, that there was something watching me, something waiting for me to falter, something just hidden in the shadows waiting to pounce. That was God. And as I fell asleep I saw the way He moved the stars out the window, felt how He heard my thoughts. I tried to be careful what I let get said up there as a kid, but it was useless. I thought of the dead man I saw once who'd been hit by a carriage and kicked by a horse, his guts showing, his head bleeding in a puddle, his leg twisted impossibly back, his smashed hand. I imagined what it felt like, and it thrilled me at first to think of that, and then it scared me. The scare was God. I knew that.

God did that, my brother had said.

When we came back from the church, our house, the whole row of houses was gone—just a pile of grey bricks and dust. I knew those church ladies had tricked us. I knew they'd killed my brother.

*A little after 3 o'clock a dreadful crash was heard; the neighbors rushed out and found that several tons in weight of the mill wall had fallen upon the roof of the Jones's store and the small homes of the mill ladies on the south-facing side of the canal. Information was immediately conveyed to the police, and every exertion was used by the neighbors to extricate those buried in the ruins. Six persons were extricated alive, namely, five children and Mrs. Jones. Several of the mill ladies and some children were pulled out in expiration.*

It's easier in the nice print, that way. I tear the paper, the newsprint, into bits and let them scatter across my lap.

I am bored to no end in this cell, and my stomach churns for something I cannot put a finger on. Not just a drink. I'd confess to anything if I could. But my head has covered everything from that night in black. That night, the lawyer is calling it. The last thing I know of Johnson is he had it in for himself, asked me again and again to help him die, and I said no and I drank hard, and I loved him. What could lead me to kill him, I don't know. If I had a drink something would open up, I'm sure. I will tell my lawyer that. I'll tell that to the judge. Someone will understand me.

Next day my lawyer comes with a hat for me to wear. He's taking me to see the judge. He asks to see what I've written.

I show him the blank paper, the unopened ink. He looks unsurprised and sits on the bed, removes his own hat, breathes deeply.

"Though I sympathize with your head problem, this malodor is really insufferable."

I don't know what to say to that.

He takes out his pipe and begins to smoke, unearthing a newspaper from my bedding and wafting the smoke around him with it.

"We can't go to the judge with nothing to say, McGlue," he says. "A plea of innocent will not get us anywhere. We'll tell him you're too sick to stand trial. That your head and your mind and body have got you too undone. We will say you are too unusual. That's what we'll do. God willing he'll at least give you more time. All you have is time from now on. You recognize that, do you?"

I nod. The lawyer is looking at my head, the dent in it. He stands up again to examine it. He takes the hat off my head and puts it down on the blank paper on the table. It will leave a brown smudge, I'm sure. His fingers in my hair poke and I wince and butt him away with my shoulder. He exhales and sits down again.

"What?" I say. He's looking at me something strange. He nods earnestly, gravely, and looks towards the wall. His one raised eyebrow tells me what to do. I walk towards the wall, turn my back, and smash my head.

He says not to wear the hat.

## Essex Street, Town Hall

*How did you become this way?*

Certain events led me to leave town, and I went south, from place to place, having my time until I met Johnson, who sort of saved me.

*What events?*

Events like what gets a man to leave his home and hitch rides down the coast and spend nights in doorways, alleys. You can make up whatever it would be for you.

The judge is a younger man than I expected. He ruffles papers for some minutes and clears his throat. The room is colder than mine, white walls chilling the air, the sunlight frozen in wide slats shooting from the high windows. I am hungry, I think. Black stars come and go. Red on my hands makes me remember. My head hurts.

*How do you explain the death of Mister Johnson?*

I can't. We were off at port and there were some jolts who took me some back place and when I came out and to the bar I got bent and woke up on board and they told me Johnson's dead, but that's just hearsay as far as I'm concerned since I ain't seen him. They blamed me for whatever happened, my captain and whoever else got to talking. Where is Johnson anyway?

*Your lawyer has insisted you are not fit to stand trial. Do you agree with his assessment? He says that you've suffered some great head trauma and suffer still. Is that accurate?*

If he means my head hurts, then yes. Nothing would bother me were someone to bring me a drink, I'd say, sir.

*Sir, I am familiar with your drink problem. Just several years ago our president spoke to the nation on the subject of your sad disease. While he said your failing should be treated as a misfortune and not as a crime or even as a disgrace, and while the court sees your misfortune, Mister McGlue, and forgives you that, your crime of murder is most appalling and must be righted. You are heretofore sent up to take residence in our jail again until your head and your mind are healed. By my best estimation six months should do it. The people of this town want a proper trial and that calls for a right-minded defendant, so get clear, sir. And the sooner the better.*

"Mister McGlue," I crack as they tie my hands again, just funny.

"They want good meat on your bones before they eat you alive," says my lawyer later.

## Howard Street, again

I've been sick again. The pillow is stained pale red and my mouth is dry. The walls of my cell are violet and blue with sundown. I watch the corners for whatever will come out of them—a kid with a bottle and change, a nice sport washermaid or some forlorn Suzie, a dog with a good stick to throw and the girl, his owner, flashing her skirts, and there's my mother in the shadows, my lawyer, and Johnson, my brother. They appear for a moment then fade back into the wall, shadows flickering as clouds pass the low moon. I suddenly have that cringey longing for a skirt. It irks me to think of my hands on what smooth, supple flesh, the stink of sugar and woman, perfume, gummy lips parting towards me, whatever I can get.

I remember something. Johnson pulling me to my knees, covering his face with his hands. It comes and goes. I think of my brother again, and my sisters.

My littlest sister was sick. "Consumption," said my mother and went to beg the mill boss to keep her job then came back with a doctor and stayed by my sister's bed for days and days. What was the big deal, I'd have liked to know. She was either all red or she was so white she was grey against the white sheet.

"Get to school, little," said my mom to me, morning, petting my sister's head, me unwashed and unfed with shoes on wrong feet and no one to walk with.

"Go to bed," she said at night after my sister was dead and carried off, by whom I didn't understand. But I wouldn't go to bed. I went out towards the pier. See if she chases me. It's early spring and my hat I don't need so I just throw it in some bushes and that makes me brave so I kick some dirt at a few horses standing outside some big gates. They wheeze and gnaw at their bits and look away like blinking fish.

"Donkeys," I say to them, and kick more dirt. Then two men come and have me by the shirt collar. They laugh and pass me back and forth, taking my face in their hands, holding me by the armpits, now throwing me up in the air.

"What's your name," they want to know.

I have my stomach hurt but I won't show it. I want to run away.

"McGlue," I tell them.

One of them pulls a silver flask from his waistcoat and leans back to drink. I see there are stains on his shirtfront, his belly's big, and his face is red and waxy in the lamplight when he takes his drag. He passes the flask to the other man. They give me a swig after all. It's my first taste of rum.

"Tastes like?"

"Taffy," I say. They give me another swig and I grab hold of the flask and duck between that fat one's splayed legs and make a run for somewhere. They let me run and laugh, but I trip and they come and kick me and take the rum back. I lay in the dirt and feel good. When I am home again my mother puts her finger to her mouth then points to the place I'm meant to sleep by the door. I go and lie down and still feel as good that time.

✢

My lawyer comes the next week with a newspaper and a letter
from my mother. She's hoping I will find the strength to carry on,
she's written, and what that looks like she has no idea. She says
she's been a widow for long enough and buried enough children to
know what real loneliness is, and says if I have any sense I will at
least confess my crime and get my wits back so they might put me
in a cell with other men, or else I will go to hell. I believe her. This
cell is good for pacing and passing out in, only that. I stand with my
back at the wall and cross my arms. My lawyer says little and pulls
another piece of paper from his case, asks me to write the story of
that night. He says that name, "Johnson."

"Where is he?" I ask. I miss him. He'd give me a bottle and talk
in a voice that would soothe, I know it. And I could rest with him
there. Though he was depressive and though he was a fool, I wish
he would visit me. My mind would work better. All my mind does
now is it spins around something I'd have sooner forgotten. Some
pointless time with nothing to it. I think of my brother some more,
try to put his face back together in my mind. His dead face in the
box, I imagine, then my sister's, then mine. I feel little.

"How are you feeling?" my lawyer asks.

I have dozed off just standing there, imagining Johnson's dead
face—blue lace beneath the pale skin, brown shirt collar too tight at
the throat so his skin is stretched and pinched and lax and that irks me.

"Fine," I answer. I can't talk. I want to. Something, a rock
maybe, is stuck in my throat.

My lawyer continues to talk about a deposition and a man named Hayes. I can barely listen. My head hurts and I look back at that dead face. I wish Johnson were here.

I remember my brother came home bleeding from the eye once. My mother put him to bed with whiskey and took me with her to the mother of the boy who did it to him. I was left to sit on a mudded stump of tree while my mother yelled at the doorway how her son could go blind, could die and leave her alone and meaningless. I was small and so often shoved off to cuddle into the nearest corner in this way, my back against some wall or other. My brother, later, didn't ask for more whiskey, just grabbed his things and went out for no trouble, then came back again unscathed.

Alone at home, I recall, it was cold almost everywhere but how exciting it was to prod at the unattended fire and let my mind go. The lights and shadows bounced around the room, caught like lightning on the windowglass and that frightened me. I threw rags on the fire and it went out.

My lawyer is now saying, "Hayes is being paid, mind you, and the longer they put you away for the more money in his pocket. So the more you stand there quietly the more free my time is. Let's talk about that night, now. Tell me what happened once you got off the boat."

"I went and borrowed some money off of Johnson. But first I walked with him and another guy around some church to take shits. I remember that because there were white nuns there guarding the door. Then Johnson borrowed me more than I asked for. I remember that."

Johnson always had the money. When he found me in New York with my head broken, his money put me in the doctor's chair. After he paid the man they sent me out and Johnson showed the doctor something of his own. I tried to listen at the door but I couldn't stand up right. What couldn't be shown in front of me, I'd have liked to know. I asked him, too, when we left the doctor's to show the captain the letter attesting to my sound health. Johnson wouldn't answer me. Then he said it was croup, which was a lie. He said it was a rash or something. He had never lied before. Of course I knew what it was. He'd put himself someplace too many other men had been before.

Poor Johnson, that fool.

And he bore the brunt of all my misdeeds. He felt what I couldn't. If he were here I'd throw an arm around him, pat his head and thank him. Whatever he'd had wrong, my wrongs were ten times the size. It was why he liked me. I think he liked to feel terrible. But he wasn't at all that way. By my side, I put him in a class of dirty animals, true, since I was one. Before me, he was a gentlemen, a person we'd despise. Once he met me, Johnson said, his heart beat a little louder. He became like a man who knew something. It helped him to have to pull me up and bring me places. And he studied my ways, tried out what it felt like to grab what was his and not apologize. Though inside, I knew, he was still so nice.

"That's a start," says my lawyer. "Write it down."

He gets up to call the guard and pulls on his coat. I find I want him to stay.

"How's the weather?" I hear myself asking.

"McGlue," he says. "It means nothing to you."

My mother cried and cried. By then I was nearly grown and had my own flask and could outrun and outhide most full-sized men, and my eyes had been blackened a few times in fights and me and Dwelly were regulars at The Long Shore and I'd been privy to a few skirts by then. None of them could draw me away from the bar for long. My mother cried every time I came through the door. Eventually I stopped coming home. Me and Dwelly got the idea to go down to Boston and be without our mothers, come to speed with life the way we wanted it. Only Dwelly wouldn't leave when it was time we said we'd leave, so I went alone.

I got a job tending horses for stagecoaches that traveled up and down to Lowell. They were ragged, unkempt animals thanks to me, and I worked with a man who was just as deep into the rum. We spent our nights in the hay, sometimes nearly freezing and watching the steamy huff and growl of the horses through the air like the clouds from a steamboat. We drank and burrowed deep into the hay and talked, some nights so cold I curled up in his arms like a kid. I don't remember his name, but he talked with the thick drawl of another country and he had the same itch as me, I remember. He talked a fair amount of women, their virtues, their stink and lather. I understood him little and it didn't matter.

What little money got handed to me in the evening, half the horses fed and languorously brushed, me half sleeping, I spent it at the Eastern Standard. There were men with money there and men without. I stood in the dark corners and watched whoever ordered rye spit and babble words, kicking up sawdust and eyeing me strangely. If there was any more money to be made I did it. These men with pocket watches, clean hands had no better way to pass the time unalone? The girls were busy, I told myself. These men's rooms were barely furnished and I didn't mind whatever they wanted. It meant another drink at last. Who could blame me? They called me Nicky Bottom. Nicky wasn't my name. McGlue I kept a secret and whistled at all the women on the street as loud as I could. There was one, another barmaid, who appeared between my arms under the gaslight on occasion. She gave free drinks, rich ones—Benedictine, Old Tom gin. My stomach was stronger then and I could drink all sorts and chew an onion and never falter. A policeman once came to me with some dollars and took me to a room, asked me to sit and watch him. I let him go on, face turning red and at the end I laughed and kicked his chair. He gave me no money after that, but it was a story to turn around in my head. Faggers, all of them. A few times I filled in on a stagecoach and saw Lowell. I could not get by there at all and was grateful for the big city with the smoke and high hats to get lost in.

I could barely read back then, I remember. Even a signpost took some force. I knew the letters and what they looked like, could have taken the time to sound them out, but unless their meaning was as obvious as "Road" or "Street" or "Town," I gave up and used my gut. It seems now that a part of my brain has been sharpened from all the booze, the hole in my head. Better to read than sit and talk, or think. My lawyer has left me yesterday's *Daily Atlas*. I look over the Merchandize column at the state of Muntz's Genuine Yellow Metal just in from Liverpool, Hydraulic Cement, better than Lime, it says, and Calf Skins, Malaga Wine, Cotton Wicking. An article advertises the sale of second-hand furniture, stoves, piano fortes and iron safes. Superb Chinese Articles—lackered and gilt—make me think of that other Christ, the turviness of one side of the world for another. I've been to China, I think. How many can boast to that? All the faces in the cold like painted on a screen, red lamps and stone, I might remember.

I might remember the harbor and the small stone walk towards a kind of inn with steaming man-sized kettles by the door, a red-and-gold painted sign swinging in the wind. It was cold. An old lady swept snow away from the door and brought us towards the fire-lit den where we sat on couches small enough to bring our knees to our chests. Girls came wrapped in layers of brittle embroidered robes and doddled in front of the fire on feet smaller than my closed fist. Their skin gleamed gold as though rubbed with fat in the firelight. Who went with which girl first I don't remember. Johnson spent a long time, I think, and came out worse than he'd gone in. I laughed at him and we slugged off to find some drink. That was good. We called it yellow wine. Then it was not so cold. We were meant to sleep back on the ship but I stayed out and Johnson came and found me in the morning. I was still up, walking like a lost dog through winding brown brick alleys, and fully frozen. Children and women came and yelled and pointed. That was Johnson. Smiling and waving and leading the way. I asked him would he like to go back to the inn and he said nothing. There was much work to do on the ship, loading and cleaning and all that. I do not miss that work a bit. Just those times with Johnson. It was hard on the ship to keep him near. When I got him to myself I was always in trouble or sick and he was mad. I was mad too. I can't remember what ever made me so mad.

It hurts my head to think of Johnson. He must be in there poking me in the brain with a long fingernail. I can imagine him crammed up in there watching with horror the rot and sludge swishing around, flapping his coat to keep it clean. I knew all his gestures, all his little kinks. When he wanted to wake me up he'd take two knuckles and grind them at my skull. A soft open palm at my chin to steady me. I try it with my own fist. It works to rewake me a little. I smell something sharp and my eyes water, my own stink suddenly as apparent as the plain, chipping walls. This is what my lawyer was talking about. A smell embroiled with whatever booze has seeped out of my body. I inhale deeply. Johnson wouldn't mind this smell. He's been through worse with me—the rank and writhing stink of sailors, tanks of spoilt fish, latrines, the blast when we removed our shirts—weeks' worth of stink there. What does my lawyer expect? That lawyer. I forget his name. I try to remember, waft the stink down towards the floor, bat the air with the folded newspaper. Let's talk, Johnson, I want to say. You saw that old man lawyer? He's all the company I have. Johnson, I say, where've you been? My lawyer said you're dead. Ha ha!

My lawyer says you're dead.

I am worried now. The guard clears his throat and his chair squeals and the sun shines through the window and I'm still breathing and I'm worried. I stare at the corner, thinking Johnson will appear, morph out of the stray shadows, take shape and come and put his hand on my shoulder. The bed shakes with just my own breathing. No Johnson. I've got it now. He is dead, just like they've been saying. I think of a drink and cry more. No kind I can think of would take the stink out of this one, though. Johnson dead. That's what they've been saying, why they've been asking. I only just heard it now. I lay my own head down and pray to die.

*Tahiti*


We have been here two days. They say the people are celebrating
the rites of spring, but it is hot as hell's summer here. I am feeling
good, supping on roast meats and dark rum enough for me to
sing in good spirits—which I've rarely done—and be among men
without loathing. There's much to enjoy here now—the short natives'
drunken dancing, the sun, the beach, the tall grasses. Johnson and I
go walking in the sugar fields, find a little bridge to rest under and
take a nap. When I wake up Johnson lays beside me like a drowned
man. His eyes are open wide. He raises himself to look down on me.
I remember this day from what he's told me.

"When we get back home," Johnson says, "I'm not living in
Salem. I'll go south, where there are fields like this, but no ocean.
I am not right like how I'm going now. I could die on this ship,
McGlue. Nothing doing but dark hearts. I would prefer to die."

He speaks like this, and as he does his face draws down like a
man twice his age. He looks at me with deploring, bloodshot eyes.

"I have money, you know," he says.

"I've figured." I nod.

This was not the Johnson who found me dead in New York,
threw me in his carriage and told me to shut up, drink and breathe.
It was not the man who tied me down with bedsheets at his sister's
and took off to do as he wanted until I was fit to walk, fuck the
world and all. He used to be like a spike-backed horse, slamming

against doors and crossing his arms and never sweating. He would melt a sword if you tried to slice him with it. In the corner, guffaw-faced and full of snit and quick to draw, that was Johnson. "Go tell it to a tree," he said every time I complained or bragged and begged. Yet everything he did to me he did to save my life. Fed me crumbs in bed nights, all I could keep down, helped me glug and didn't deny me any kind of drink. "I've got a dream of us on the high water," he'd said. He made it happen. He was like that—burning with want and courage, drunk that way. I had so much in kin with him, drunk on drink and supped and with my mouth full of deep meaning, drooling, head half caved-in from my fall from the train. He had changed full round from that dolt who came across me freezing in the woods outside New Haven. He had become, truth be told, a kind of monster. He talked of killing his father, wrath and bloodlust wrinkling his fine brow. "You've helped me," he always said. I knew what he meant. Fuck the world and go on, that was what I taught him. It seems he's fallen from his own train as now he shakes his face, blurries his eyes, smears tears away with the cuff of his unbuttoned shirt. "McGlue?" he asks, with nothing to follow it. Johnson would have dug his hands into my brain to pull out that one so rusted spring. But no. Bent and sore and dampened with gloom, this is not that man.

We have been here three days. Today the men balk at the train of costumed townspeople, drink from the jug directly, spit, sling one another over their newly regalia-ed backs and run towards the whorehouse. Johnson and I go with them. It's a little bronze-brown shanty, freshly repainted for the holiday. They sit behind the curtain on

a rattan bench full of cockroaches. The curtain is embroidered with
the traditional flora and seaspray—red and pink flowers, a stilled
crashing wave caught open-mouthed, spitting blue beams of yarn.
Each time one man comes out and another goes in, all of us stand
and shake hands. I laugh at each of them and get soft punches to my
shoulders in retaliation, wait my turn. It is a bright and wasted day.
An orange dog lingers at the doorway. Johnson gets up to pet it.

"He'll have the dog," says one of the men to the fat, brown
mother.

Johnson kneels down to look into the dog's eyes. Because I
know he had a winsomeness about the canines, I don't bother him.

"Maybe he's already had the dog," another of the men goes on.

I am no longer surprised at Johnson's steady failures with the
women. He gets forlorn and angry when it's over with, won't stand
for conversation. I've teased him a few times and got his grit teeth
and flared up face and silence for the next few days. He's even
thrown a punch, which I laughed at. I just keep quiet now. Now I'm
up. I stand and ask the fagger to hold my knife. He comes along,
sometimes, and will watch through a curtain in return for however
many bottles I think it's worth. I do it all just for sport.

Later Johnson and I go back to the ship and sit on the bow,
watch the skies needlessly for storm, drinking. Johnson stares out
at the scant clouds with the seriousness of a man who prays. The
captain is sleeping below deck. The ship sways and kicks in the
harbor. Johnson takes out his knife and licks the blade. I just sit
and watch him. He spits blood at the rushing foam. I take out my

rigging knife and cut my gums on the metal tang, tasting it to see whatever it is Johnson would believe tastes good, or tastes of something.

He is irritated. Behind him the island is paved with gold and spices and this is supposed to be his lot but he's not been interested in our work for days. He says he feels little for these men. They are young and dragonny, pretentious and dull like that, and they think he's wry and darkhearted and beleaguered, to be pitied and feared. He tells me all this and spits at the grey harbor. I watch him and suck from the bottle alone, thinking how the man must need a special kind of whore, or something else, I don't know. Then Johnson takes up the knife again and throws it at the water. It flickers with sunshine as it nicks the surface, glitter splashing up into his eyes like something happy, like springtime. But he just rubs his eyes with the butts of his palms and looks down. Our reflection juts and quivers on the water.

He stands and quickly dives. The knife he finds raveled up in sea weeds, he claims. He climbs the anchored rope back on board, has another idea so then takes off his wet boots and jumps up and walks along the boom gripping the knife between his teeth and shimmies up the mast. Splayed like a bat, he fists the mainsail in his hands and, hanging by one arm, cuts and tears down what he can. The holes in the sails don't add up to much. When he gets back down he daubs at the corners of his mouth for blood with the torn-down sail, wipes the knife clean on his pantleg, and charges off across the warm stone plaza, barefoot, into the town.

It might be my fate to follow him out there, but the sea is moving so nicely, it feels good to watch it and be quiet, let the rum take root

and warm my bones. Johnson calls to me, "McGlue!" I'm more of
a watchdog for him these days than him for me. Someone to point
things out to, frown to, to be ready with a rude joke. It worries me
for a minute to think of Johnson out there, alone, his knife primed
and no one to turn to in this strange place. But the sun is shining
and for once I can breathe. Why? This rum is good. Strange ale is all
we've had onboard for weeks.

I recall my first time with a lady. The smell of it like cooking
cabbage. What claims I've ever made to loving a woman scorned
is just a half-truth. I love them most when they are suffering awful
and full of wrath. I like to play certain games. My hands at their
throats is a good one—all that soft, gristly stuff to squeeze. This
whore here on the island was a little one—shy and naked sitting
with her back towards me when I walked in. I don't take my clothes
off, just go to the chair and unbuckle my belt. There is one way to
do it, then another. I try not to see her face. Her narrow hips are
stiff and strangely askew in my lap, her back flounced over like
a limp flower. "Good enough," I say after a while, stand up and
leave. This was yesterday. The other men rile and jack and slap each
other's backsides and boast and tell stories. I listen because I like to.
Johnson just walks away.

Johnson at the whorehouse in Victoria. A fat one with rings of
gold in her nose and ears. That wasn't any good. Johnson got mad
and left. I saw his vest just one button undone. And Johnson at the

whorehouse in Cape Town. Somewhere we'd never been before, flesh like hot meat pulled from a grill. He stormed out and grabbed my arm. "Don't go in there," he said. "I don't want to know what you'd do with that." But I went in anyway, tossed the girl around in ways I found funny, then went out back and smoked a pipe some old man passed me. That was good.

And Johnson at the whorehouse in Salem. Some lady's parlour back on St Ides Street above a shop that sold nothing I'd ever buy. The girls upstairs had hair of all different colors. Johnson took the black-haired one. A pretty thing with pale skin and dark, protruding eyes, a dark brow. But that wasn't good enough either.

"What are you expecting? At least take some fun out of them," I said to him.

He just shrugged his shoulders and pulled me by the shirtsleeve. He was rather for getting into fights those days. Anything, it seemed, could put him out of himself, ally his fist with the rough edge of another man's jaw. That I understood. There were better things than women. I had my own misgivings, too.

Like something about a suckling baby drove me ten yards. Something about that kind of memory. My mother with my sister in a sling. My brother passing her whatnot and me in the corner, covering my ears and gagging. That hot spurt of what passed as love, my mother. The first thing I hate about women is that smell.

"Move it, little," she said when I got in her way, and I got in her way often. I was always "little," never called by my right name, which I barely remember at this point.

"McGlue," Johnson says grabbing his jacket and moving towards the whorehouse door. "Let's go find someone to beat."

When Johnson turns up again it is in a maelstrom in the waters of a bay a good ten minute walk from where I've last seen him on the ship. Deep enough into the water but not too far for us not to see him, he's yelling at me to save him, churning the thick waves with his arms. Somehow I know this is all for show. What man wades willingly so deep into water that he must be saved? Surely his mind is gone. I won't swim out there. Salted water, like all things that go into wounds, fills my skull, makes me dizzy and dead.

"Get on out there," I yell to the men. They go, casting off their jackets and hats and boots, each man outsplashing the next for who can get to Johnson first. I watch with my hands in the sand, feeling around, still the warm sun on my face. I feel almost like an angel here. Later I'll eat a jar of honey, I think. Whatever sweet stuff I can find. Wine would be good. Some kind I've never had before. But when they pull Johnson out of the water he staggers and spits and his eyes are red and he falls at my side and pants.

"I could have drowned," he tells me.

"I've drowned lots of times," I say back to him.

He lays his head down on the sand and closes his eyes. The men circle and wait, dripping like rain, also panting.

I'm not averse to calling him the chickenshit he is, but not so soon. I think he's earned a little bit of this show. And I do take it as a show. The real Johnson wouldn't be so nancy. He'd spit at the foot of any knee-fallen man, spit on his gooey eyes and walk away. This Johnson here is like a whiny baby.

"I almost died, McGlue," he's saying, one hand crawling up my ankle and gripping my calf, as though that would comfort him.

"You poor soul," I say, laughing. I wrest my leg free and kick him not so hard in the ribs.

"Get up, Johnson," I tell him. And he does. I decide not to tease him anymore. We walk together back to the ship in silence.

In the morning he claims it was just something he ate. Claims to barely remember, but still asks me, what I take as a joke time after time, to put him out of his misery.

But I would not kill Johnson. He liked to be jostled, though. If he were here I'd punch his face till he laughed. He got jolly, punch-drunk. I was good at cheering him when I got tight the right way, which wasn't often. It was after a dry spell, when the ship ale tasted all right.

"Tell me a joke, Mick," he'd say.

"Let's get the fagger in here and have some fun."

That fag had seen all sorts from us. We'd make him drop his pants and stick it in a bottle. "Drink this, Johnson," I'd make him do. It produced in him, Johnson, a great hysteria. "Put this up you know what," I'd tell the fag. That got me, too. Sometimes I wanted to slam him against the wall with the bottle in him, crush it, watch him bleed.

But that fag was in charge of the booze. Insofar as he enjoyed these tricks I played on him, I couldn't go too far, couldn't blacken his eyes too badly. But Johnson and I knew he wanted us both, the wrong way. It kept us from each other, Johnson and me, from talking too closely when we bunked side by side on a cold night on the ship. Just that idea in the air between us.

"This is a good start," my lawyer says. The praise fills me with disgust somehow. I beat my head with my fists.

"You can call me Foster," is all he says.

"Foster," I call him.

He's brought me a book to read. It's that book.

"If anything strikes you, you tell me about it," he says, and bangs on the bars to wake the guard. Before he goes he feels my skull. Soft, wrinkled fingers parting my hair tenderly. I think to grab his arm and slam him, but the temptation leaves me fast. It's a kind of tenderness I don't know. It makes me feel sick to my stomach.

"You're getting better," he says, nudges the book towards me across the table and leaves.

But I don't feel good. I feel like sleeping, a white light entering my vision like a torch of sunlight to my brain. Like an arrow on fire. I haven't felt the sun really in months. It's near dark outside. The window shows a grey, pitiless sky, which is nice, I think. I watch the room darken, crinkling the newspaper Foster has left me on the table, next to that book.

The date startles me. Only so few days since I've been put in this cell, hair already grown and cut, so many bottles gone undrunk. There's a kind of fixing of my eyes on the small print like ants on a bleached stone floor.

"Poisoned and pernicious as the American character may be, yet there is not a breeze that sweeps across the ocean but that brings on it tidings of woe, more startling than any thing that springs up in our own land."

For good measure, I open the book Foster has left me. I want to see if God himself will guide my finger to an answer. The question being why the woe, why such tidings? Why not just the breeze and the ocean? Why me?

"And when you stand praying, if you hold anything against anyone, forgive him."

I stand. I stand praying, just to see what happens. All I know to do is put my hand on my heart. There's no real evil there, I'm sure. But it is empty.

"Johnson," I say to the dark room now. "Come and bring me a keg or two, let this woe-be-gone go and tell me a joke, something. Anything," I say.

For good measure I hit myself upside the skull. I think to say a real prayer, and almost do. Johnson always told me to wish on my own hands, not the stars. I think of this. I kiss each of my fingers, watch the newspaper drift like the wings of a tired bat to the floor.

And he appears.

He's got on a red jacket and a hat I'll make fun of. But his face is already laughing.

"McGlue," he says, "you bully trap. Why so soft?"

"I've grown two inches since they threw me in here. Can you get me out?"

"I do have money," he answers. He's just a flipping arrangement of lights that my blurred eyes put together. I know that.

"They say I killed you," I say to him anyway.

I have to keep twisting my vision, pulling at my lids with my fingers, for him not to disappear.

"You did, McGlue," says Johnson. "I'm sorry," he says.

"Are you mad?" I ask.

"I'm not mad," he says. "Though I wish you'd join me."

He's gone. A grey, cooing pigeon is left in his wake, shifting uneasily, carefully folding its wings, seated on the corner of my bed.

## Port David

If I am to write about what's ailed me, I'll go here.

What country I'm in, I don't know. I'm awake on a road. I've
come to on my feet, striding towards a clock tower. My shadow is
cast long and dark and bends with the toss of my head and jolt of
step towards something. It's my head swaying and cursing. I have
horns, I feel like. The chirr of hidden insects twitters like a snake in
the grass. I still don't know where I am.

Someone calls out. To me, I don't know. The language might
be my own but I can't make out the words. A bell dongs how many
times. People come out from a shadowed pavilion somberly wearing
white gloves, suits, wide-brimmed hats. How am I to know where to
hide? The sun bounds out like a man for the punch.

"Gringo," a small child says, and points. I make out his face. A
smile twisted down in scorn.

I've heard this word before. It means I am some kind of devil.
The Devil himself, maybe. "I know him well," I'd like to say. "But I
am not that."

And now I know where I am. I go on in search of more. The
light is getting to my head, I'm almost crying. Through a break in
the plaza I see the harbor. That's where I should go. But first, a drink.

I pass an alley where the sun doesn't shine. Promising. The smell
is distinct against the sunlit dust and nothing. The door is just an
old piece of wood propped up against the jam. Already from outside

I see the long bar, the bottles, the haunch and hunch of those sitting, nursing. One pounds on the bar for another. This is where I am.

I walk in and no one turns to look at me. I stand at the bar and wait for the man's attention. He ignores me.

Then I see him at the table. His hat is on. I know him. It's Johnson. Without asking I know he is here because it's how he'd find me, at the bar.

"Buy me a drink, fartcatcher," I say nearly toppling the table when I punch his shoulder.

He says something I don't understand and a girl comes with two bottles. Johnson puts one in his pocket and slides the other into my open hands.

"We're leaving," he says.

"Fine with me."

I glug one bottle down and leave it spinning on the table. Johnson says, "Wait till the ship to drink the other."

"One more for the way," I say.

He gets two more from the bar and we go back into the dark alley, me drinking across the sunsoaked plaza towards the harbor. On board, I don't remember the map of the ship. I keep walking into ropes and boxes, the wood-panelled ends of hallways downbelow.

"No fimble-famble," I hear. It's the captain. He looks fresh shaved. My own face is covered in little wires that amount to nothing but the look of dirt. It is a kind of dirt, things that grow out from me. It means I have dirt deep inside of me. A head full of dirt, maybe. When I've had a few, nice soft dirt. Otherwise I am livewired, hungry-eyed like

a scorned wolf, but give the appearance of a nervous boy, tittering
along in search of something, namely, another drink.

It's boring to go on like this. The lawyer knows who I am.
I am a drunk.

It took me some time to know this.

Here is how I know. How it's always been is I don't know how
to talk or move or sleep or shit. I wake up mornings with my head
in a vice. The only solution is to drink again. That makes me almost
jolly. It does wonders in the morning to take my mind off the pain
and pressure. I can use my eyes after that first drink, I remember
how to line up my feet and walk, loosen my jaw, tell someone to
get out of my way. Then I get tired. I whine and need to lie down.
I lie down, I want a drink. I cannot sleep without having already
forgotten my name, my face, my life. If I were to sit still or lie down
in a room with some memory of myself—the time I have left to live
out, that nasty sentence, that hell—I would go mad. My work on the
ship is a joke, sometimes made to dump water leaked in through a
hole like in my head, sometimes forced back to bed to bleed, they
call it. Why they haven't thrown me overboard yet, I am waiting.
It's Johnson who is mad, the way he looks at me, ignores me, comes
to me at night with his face covered in tears and snot saying, "I am
mad." Or not mad. Maybe I am mad. My mother says I am the son
of the Devil. How could she be wrong?

## Salem

I've made the papers. It is written, first page, everything—my aberrant behavior, my arrogant denial, my questionable manhood, and so on. They compare me to a dog without a single moral bone of his own to gnaw. They say the judge should have me put down, they call it. Put down where? I want to know. There couldn't be a place any more down than this jail cell. Besides the one jaunt to the courthouse I haven't felt fresh air on my face in months. Nobody handing me a drink, a toast: "To the Republic." I sometimes hear the guards making jokes, laughing. I hear a chair creaking as one leans back, scratches his heads, yawns. They must check the clock to see how many more hours they have to sit there, minding I don't kill myself. Time. How much longer till they pick up their coats and walk out into the world. That kills me. It is hard not to want to die. Already I am waning here day after day. I exercise my face at times so as not to go cripple, not to forget how to smile or frown. Otherwise I have only slack cheeks and mouth, the loose rung of my jaw swinging as I turn my head from side to side.

Foster comes once every few days to collect my confessions. He does not seem displeased, though he says I paint too detailed a picture. "We won't throw them out," he says. He seems to be getting a gist of Johnson, and I worry I have painted him too flimsy, like a rich boy with no backbone. I should right that. Foster will want me to right that. I have told him that I have been having visions, hearing voices. He says he prays these are signs of my memories healing my brains back together. "But," he says. "Be kind to those visitors. If you rile them, they may wreak havoc nobody knows."

Now I must think of Johnson. The beloved son with an inheritance and good breeding and the handsome face like a picture selling gold. The face of a man who could convince you of anything's worth. He often spoke of the value of things, what their costs were versus how much went into making them. Pocket watches and fine coats, books and hats, a fine wine. "I want to know where things come from," he told me. He had much more knowledge of the world, the map of it. He told me there were diamonds the color of blood, mermaids, herbs that could give a man eternal life. Me, peddling my legs around Salem like a windup doll looking for a glass teat to suck. "We'll go," he said. "I'd even pay my way." But he didn't have to try hard to get a job on that ship, and with him me too. Looking like a stowaway I made onto that ship the day of departure with Johnson clearing a path for me, like a prince. "He's not feeling well," was his explanation for why I was stained with wine, stumbling, smirking and raising a finger to say something, then forgetting and stumbling on.

"Put him to bed," Johnson said to the fagger whenever I had to lean over the railing to vomit or got struck by the rock of waves and lay down flat on the deck. That small-handed fag tapped on the pillow and smoothed my hair. I miss getting laid up like that, being put to bed. Johnson came in eventually to survey my progress. He tucked me in right. Put a cool hand on my forehead, rolled down my eyelids with the tips of his fingers like laying a corpse to rest. He was tender. He could be so tender sometimes, even when he was striding around like some prize horse. He never gripped me hard or steered me away. He told me it wasn't my fault each time I'd fall off the crumbling wagon. "Try again," he said. I'd nod and smile, then slip on a patch of ice on the road soon as we docked, hit my head good and talked to the stars. Every night he'd say it. "Try again tomorrow."

"Oh yes," I told him. "Tomorrow. Just one last drink." He never denied me. I cannot understand how he did it—he always had a bottle in his pocket just for me.

Foster is a poor substitute for my old dead friend. His newspapers make good gifts, that's true. Yesterday's had a little drawing of me—my face on a large rattish body, small horns, dragging a weed-strewn anchor by my ankle. The face I'm giving is sharp-toothed and thin and like a starving fox. At least they are not too far off there. It gives me a little joy to see my name printed in those same black marks as the President, the date, the state of Massachusetts. Here now the news is much more exciting than days' past. Men and women shot in the heads in Mexico, a message sent by magnetic telegraph, a warning to mariners of winds that will carry you to hell, how many dissolutions of partnerships. Reading can consume me for a while, broadening my eyes in a way I need to spite my small cell. A girl with a tail stuns a local parishioner. And then a long column on the Negroes. I haven't thought of them in months. The old ones on the boat just shied in and out of rooms, barely creaking the wood plank floors. And here they are discussed in detail. Their plight and brand, all that labor. There is justice for some. A whole color of people set free and me still in here to rot until I go mad enough to believe I am the murderer they say I am, and even then. Though Johnson did appear and has told me I've done it. I can't believe that. He just won't admit he's done it to himself, I imagine. I will propose that to Foster. Johnson did himself in, of course. There might be no refuting that one.

I go back to bed with some relief and sleep despite a gnawing itch at the open back door of my broken head.


It's not easy to breathe beneath the dingy violet skies of late evening. That color lurks from the window and into my gut through my eyeballs and pithies and churns up what should be just a watery reserve of tears. Salem turns my sorrow into a thick glue. It is what stuck me to Johnson, I am thinking. For those purple skies with black birds lacing up from black huddled branches of the city park and careening across the flat plane of space which ends just at my window ledge, I have thought more than once how to break the glass. But there are bars against it, and breaking it would only serve to let in wind and snow and rain. This blanket here, the one Foster gave me, has saved me many nights from freezing. Or so it feels. The cold current of prison air. After a few months even, the thought of a drink gets me first hot and annoyed, then cold and shaking. It's been going on. If only a drink would surface from any of my now scant apparitions, that would be good. I do still think often of a drink. I know all the bars in Salem and all the ways around the roads towards them and back home again like clockwork—even blind I could find my way, and have. If I could fly, that would be good. I call out to Johnson to appear again. He doesn't. Too soon, maybe, since his last visit. I call out for someone, anyone to appear. I get a strange creature curled in the corner. It flaps a hand back at me like to swat away a fly.

Who is this? I wonder.

I am your conscience, I hear it say in my own voice.

A few nights later, a cool hand on my head lifts me from sleep. It is Johnson. He has brought a mirror, a sharp broken blade of glass he pulls from his pocket. A small rendition of my face appears in the reflection, my breath like smoke in the cold dribbling from my lips. I look dead. Johnson appears solid this time. He lays the mirror by me on the bed and crosses his arms. His height startles me—so big and strong, not like the last of his days as I remember them. He became whittled down to my size in his lament, his woe. This is the old Johnson back again.

"Are you better now?" I ask him. He doesn't answer—only a shrug. He looks off at the hallway through the bars. "I think I've been duped," I tell him. "What are you doing here?"

I am awake now, or I am not awake at all. My head has cleared, my vision so well lit it's as if someone has set the scene—moonlight through the barred windows, the black curtain of night hanging in the room behind Johnson, now down on one knee beside me, face cast in half-shadow. He shows me the sharp edge of the broken mirror again, and with that I hear him say without words, "You killed the wrong man."

I guess it's true. I'm sorry I'm not dead. There must be something funny in me. "I often did what ought to be done the other way around." I try to laugh. "It's my spoilt brains, Doctor Johnson. Are you here to pull them out, throw the rotten mess in the sea for the sharks to eat?" It hurts to look at him, so stiff. "I will do it myself," I tell him, and get my hand up at the back of my head, and poke and pry, and some hair and dried blood come off between my fingers.

"I need a knife," I say. I feel under the mattress for the one Foster gave me but it isn't there. Johnson hands me the shard of mirror. It is real in my hand as I stab and prod best I can, even as Johnson leans back against the cold prison walls, watching. The crack in my skull isn't wide enough to anchor in and pry it open, but I try. It hurts good. Blood drips from my nose onto the pale woolen blanket. I keep working, dedicated now to see what's inside. But my arm will not bend the way I need it to. Johnson is in the corner now, covering his eyes with his sleeve. I call to him to help me get inside myself. The guard groans and I hear the clink of his keys as he walks. Johnson hides somewhere. In the meantime, I've made some progress. My hands are hot and wet with blood.

When I awake the next morning I am not in my cell.

"You died, McGlue," Foster is saying, hovering above my feet in a gold-buttoned jacket. Or "You have not died," he is saying. A yellow light shoots around my eyes, and I am crying.

"Are you crying?" he asks me.

"What?"

"You did a stupid thing," he says.

"Thank God," I say. And I do not know what I am saying. My hands are not shaking, and my mind is not blackened with whatever had done it so much damage, but I cannot say how I am changed. I turn to look at Foster. Light and music surround him. There is much I'm not shown by my eyes and instead a song, a woman's voice.

It is my mother.

"You stupid child," she says, setting down a bag of bread. "They come to tell me my son has killed hisself and when I get here, here you are. Can you hear me? They say you, what, were trying to touch your brains. Filthy."

It's a song she's sung before, I think. Foster moves away from the window. My eyes blacken with dread. My mother bangs the bread on the table. But it is not bread. Just a swollen fist wrapped in a brown rag.

"Your hand, ma?"

"It wasn't smart, they will delay the hearing," Foster says.

Whose hands in whose bandages, I am dreaming of something I've seen before, or done.

"They say your brains were spilling out. How you are not dead, God knows."

"Only God would know that," says my mother. She pulls taffy from a bag and throws it into the air. Where is it landing? Foster sits and waits for the bandages to come off my head. He wants to inspect me.

"As soon as we get to the truth, we'll have something to rely on. You must be tied down for the time being." He sits and gets up and sits and regards my mother with long-drawn, suspicious eyes. She offers him a buttered roll. Something is going on.

"I'm sorry about my son," my mother says.

The room swells and hums with something. God has not forsaken me, I am thinking. And then I am thinking, I have God. I hadn't had it, and now I do. I mean to tell Foster but he has left the room. I cannot move my arms or legs. They must be tied down. I cannot lift my head. I am not forlorn or angry. I put myself at ease with a song.

And then I am alone in the room.

And then they are back again, drowning the voice in my head with their banter.

"Such and this and that," they say. They sound like an engine blowing. The long toot of a ship at harbor.

If I've killed Johnson it must have been done at night, mistakenly, with my hand wielding some showy knife in jest, and Johnson come up behind it.

"By now it means nothing, McGlue," says Foster. But before he's said the truth meant everything. "Either they will find you mad and lock you up forever, or they will find you mad and release you to your mother, like a dumb little child."

My mother darns a sock and mourns. She's seen her house crumble down on her most-loved son, she's saying. I tell Johnson and Foster, this mother is not in my head. I have seen her with my own eyes. She is a darkhearted bitch. See her now? She is sitting there, spitting on my grave.

Johnson says, "I died early morning." Foster can't see him. Maybe my voice has said it, though I feel breath on my neck. I'm sitting in a proper chair now. Foster is by the door, watching me. My mother is doing dishes. My brother writes in a book and spills the ink.

"That's all right," says my mom.

"That's all right."

"We're rich," someone says.

"He's left you a fortune."

"It's true," says Foster. "Enough for your life story."

My mother wears a crown of gold and spits on my grave and cries.

"If I killed Johnson, it was his careless fault. He just fell towards me. He could never hold his liquor. He fell on the sword, as they say."

We'd always been good friends, remember. He saved my life. I was freezing to death somewhere, nearly a stone statue with icicles hanging from my nose. On a horse he came up promising me what, I forget now, again.

"Safe travels."

"That's right."

"That's all right," says Foster.

"Sleep now." I sleep now. In the morning angels sing my burial march.

In the morning I remember everything. And there is Johnson at my neck, lips tender and wrestling, nearly at my throat, saying, "And then what? In the morning, what happened, once we got there, and I stopped you, and I said what?"

He means the day in Stone Town when he died. I can barely think.

A nurse brings me a pot to piss in. The fagger rubs my chest with salve. The sun is quickly blotted out by storm through the window and

FENCE ⟫ BOOKS

ACKNOWLEDGMENTS

The author wishes to thank
Susan Collyer, Brian Evenson,
Rivka Galchen, Rebecca Wolff,
Bill Clegg, and Jean Stein.

Selections from *McGlue* have appeared
in *LIT* and *Electric Literature*.

THE END

"I love you," he says again.

At the docks there is a nigger girl in rags dealing red flowers. I buy one and tuck it in my hair behind my ear. The men dog me and I dance a jig. My mother covers her eyes.

"We were in the plaza. You pulled me aside, into a dark alley. This was sun-up. You said you had decided to die. You remember this."

"You or me?" I ask. "One of us has to go," one of us says.

His knife is pretty and he says, "Just go ahead and do it." My rigging knife is rusty and he sees it and says, "Just go on."

But first.

*And all the times we'd said we'd loved you,* the songs always went.

"And I kissed you. And the knife went in."

And we kiss then and there, and maybe I die then first of all. Right away, though, instead of lips a fist soars into my mouth, for which I am grateful. Johnson says it again, "Go ahead," and I smear my bloody mouth on his.

Shaking under the sun and clouds, clear-headed and shaded in sweat and furious, I look down at his face, the gleaming black sunlit hair, hear him say my name once more, and so I kneel to kiss him. I raise the knife again.

I'm facedown again in the hay-filled pillow, feeling the ship rock, my head heavy, my fingertips swollen, Johnson in and out to check, saying each time he leaves, "He's sick, don't bother him," having left me with another bottle of rum.

Here comes that fag for the last time. This time I am a murderer and he looks at me funny. Give me some of that, I want to say, but my arm, which I mean to raise to point a finger before my jaw opens to say it, is tied down. Who is responsible for this act of kidnap, I'd like to ask. I am drunk. Outside the stars spin so beautifully. Johnson appears like a vapor, moves quickly through the room and gets into bed with me. "Johnson," I say. "Don't be a fag." He's covered with blood and his eyes gape wide in horror. He's a corpse. And outside the sun is shining, and the moon wanes and dawns. At night the stars spin and sparkle, then drift. Foster tells me to look straight and say what I can see. Pen-and-ink pictures meant for children. "Dog," "Train," "House," is as far as I go with no wrong answers. "Minute," "Fairly," "Tell you," "But first."

On the boat the fagger comes to bed with me.

"I love you," he says. And I am dreaming. A few silver pieces are shoved in my pocket. My mouth stirs. Johnson meets me in the street outside. It is Zanzibar. It is New York City.

"I have a fortune," Johnson says. He hands me a few silver pieces. I go into the shop and buy a bottle.

"One bottle at a time," says the man behind the counter.

I go outside and back in again. He sells me another.